Will motioned for his reluctant partner to join him.

"What's your name?"

"Mel…uh, short for Melody," she answered softly.

"Okay, class, Melody is going to help me demonstrate proper frame. Square up with your partner like this," Will said, as he began his explanation of the proper dance positions.

Normally, Will could recite this spiel in his sleep, but today he was struggling to concentrate. There were too many variables splitting his attention. First, he had to keep his eye on the rest of the class to be sure they were keeping up. Next, he had to help his timid partner who was fighting him every step of the way. And finally, he was trying to keep his hands from sliding off her tiny top to her bare skin.

"Not so much resistance, Melody," he murmured in her ear. Then, louder to the class, he said "Ladies you should be pushing against the leader's shoulder *lightly*. Keep in mind we're dancing not wrestling."

ROBYN AMOS

worked a multitude of day jobs while pursuing a career in writing after graduating from college with a degree in psychology. Then she married her real-life romantic hero, a genuine rocket scientist, and she was finally able to live her dream of writing full-time. Since her first book was published in 1997, Robyn has written tales of romantic comedy and suspense for several publishers, including Kensington, Harlequin and HarperCollins. A native to the Washington, D.C., metropolitan area, Robyn currently resides in Odenton, Maryland.

Enchanting
MELODY

ROBYN AMOS

I would like to thank my critique partners, Judy Fitzwater, Pat Gagne, Ann Kline and Karen Smith, who have been by my side since the very beginning. Special thanks to my silent critique partner and husband, John Pope. I'd also like to thank my pre-wedding dance instructors, Clifford Kopf, Anne Arundel Community College, and Deborah Joy Malkin, First Dance Impressions.

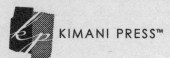 KIMANI PRESS™

ISBN-13: 978-0-373-86018-0
ISBN-10:   0-373-86018-8

ENCHANTING MELODY

Copyright © 2007 by Robyn Amos

www.kimanipress.com

Printed in U.S.A.

Dear Reader,

I got the idea for *Enchanting Melody* while I was planning my wedding. My husband and I decided to warm up for our first dance with ballroom dancing lessons at the local community college. I took one look at our handsome dance instructor—debonair Fred Astaire by night, investment banker by day—and knew he was a romance novel waiting to happen.

Enter Will Coleman, Wall Street stockbroker and part-time fox-trotter, and Melody Rush, reluctant maid of honor and captive dance student. Even the toughest woman's resolves melt when a suave gentleman twirls her in his arms like a ballerina—something Melody learns, much to her dismay.

These two are from different worlds. Will is climbing to the top of the ivory tower from the wrong side of the tracks. Melody is rushing down from the penthouse to mingle with Goths. But when they meet in each other's arms on the dance floor, magic happens.

My husband and I eventually signed up for private lessons and found that learning to dance could be a real test of a couple's relationship. Yes, I was one of those women who always wanted to lead. But I finally learned that dancing is like love. You have to know when to lead, know when to follow and trust your partner to hold up their end of the bargain.

I love to hear from readers. E-mail me at robynamos@aol.com or visit me on the Web at www.robynamos.com.

Happy reading!

Robyn Amos

Chapter 1

Melody Rush tossed her waist-length ponytail over her shoulder as she squinted at the drawing board.

"That's not quite what I'm looking for, Bass," she told her friend, a hulking goth with blood-red streaks in his black hair. "Can you arch your back a little more?"

"If I arch it any more, I'm going to fall on my head. I'm defying gravity as it is," he moaned. Arms outstretched, head thrown back, Bass struggled to contort his spine as though reeling from a powerful blow.

Melody tried to sketch faster, realizing she was wearing out her model—which is why she didn't typically rely on them to develop her comic-book characters. "I'm sorry, dude, but this was your idea, remember?"

For years, Bass had been begging to be the inspiration for a character in one of her graphic novels. Finally, Delilah, her flashy African-American heroine—supermodel by day, electrically-charged crime fighter by night—had beaten up all the local villains and was in need of a fresh archenemy.

"I remember," he paused to groan. "But, I thought I'd at least get in a few good licks. So far, in *all* these poses Delilah is kicking my—"

"Bass, I've already told you, the Ambassador's power is primarily cerebral. After this colossal butt-kicking he concocts a mind-control spell to take over the world."

"Yeah, whatever. Can't I hit her just once?"

Melody shot him a look, pointedly ignoring the question. "Okay, you can relax. I think I've got what I need." Her pencil flew over the sketch pad in rapid strokes that finally ended in a flourish.

The chains looped through his wide-leg jeans rattled as he straightened. "You ever notice that Delilah's enemies are always men?" he asked, cracking his neck. "If you're not careful, your fans will start to think you're a man-hater."

"Hah, I'm far from a man-hater," she said, waving him off.

"I don't know, you're much nicer now that we're not dating. But, I still think you're using Delilah to express your pent-up aggression toward men." Bass was forced to take a hasty step back as Melody surged to her feet.

"I do not have pent-up aggression." Sticking one hand on her hip, she waved the index finger of her other hand in the air. "First, I've *always* been nice—you just didn't know how to stand up to me. Second, Delilah is not an extension of me. In fact, she's my polar opposite."

"Opposite?" Bass snorted. "Come on, she has the same brown skin tone as you, the same unbelievably long hair, and she's tall and curvy, just like you."

She answered the lascivious arching of his brow with a hard glare. "Physical similarities mean nothing. Delilah's a girly-girl. I'm a tomboy. She wears Prada suits and Jimmy Choo shoes. I wear cargo pants and army boots. I'm sick of people trying to draw a connection between Delilah and me. She's *completely* fabricated."

Except, maybe, for her hair. It was Melody's only true vanity. She'd given Delilah her trademark waist-length hair because she was so proud of it. Though she most often kept it in a braid or ponytail streaming down her back, she was meticulous when it came to grooming it.

"Fine, don't blame me just because you're bound by the dark chains of denial."

She rolled her eyes, sitting back down at her desk. "Don't be so melodramatic."

He took a step toward her. "Never mind. Can I see how I turned out?"

"Not yet," she said, covering the drawing. "I need to play with it a bit more."

"Fine, but, for all my effort, you've got to give me something." Bass, topping six feet with the build of a heavyweight wrestler, rubbed his hands together like an eager little boy. "How about giving the Ambassador X-ray vision? I'm dying to see what Delilah wears under that catsuit."

Melody started to quip that he wouldn't be able to handle it, but was interrupted by the telephone.

She crossed the room and glanced at the caller ID—it was her sister.

As much as she loved her younger sibling, she wasn't in the mood to discuss fabric samples or cake flavors for Stephanie's upcoming wedding.

After the fourth ring, she answered the line. "What's up, Steph?"

"Get ready to buzz me in, I'm a block away from your apartment, and I've got a present for you."

Melody sighed, hanging up the phone. These days that could mean a lot of things, and none of them good.

"My sister's on her way up here, Bass. You may want to hit the road." Her sister and her best friend detested each other.

Bass rolled his eyes and grabbed his skateboard. "I'm outta here. Have fun drinking tea with the diva."

The doorbell rang and Mel buzzed her sister through the security doors in the lobby. Moments later, Stephanie breezed into the apartment, filling it with expensive perfume. Casual only by design, she wore denim capri pants with a short denim jacket as a top. She'd completed her outfit with high-heeled sandals and pearls.

Stephanie Rush had retired from runway modeling to plan her New York wedding full-time. If it weren't for the fact that they lived on opposite sides of the city, Melody would've had to tolerate these pop-ins once a day.

As it was, they came at least once a week—every time Stephanie changed her wedding theme, colors or guest list.

"Hey, girl." Stephanie leaned in to kiss Melody on the cheek before sitting next to the large portfolio she'd propped against the couch. "I just passed Flounder in the lobby."

"Bass."

"Right, I knew it was a fish. How is it that a thirty-year-old man still rides a skateboard?"

"Don't knock it." Melody had learned to ignore her sister's none-too-subtle digs at her friends. "Skateboards are fuel-efficient, environmentally-friendly and good exercise."

"Whatever. Guess what? I have a surprise for you," Stephanie said in a singsong voice.

Mel braced herself. "Okay?"

Stephanie reached into her Louis Vuitton bag and handed Melody a white envelope. Mel took it and pulled out what looked like a gift certificate.

"This coupon entitles you to six ballroom-dancing lessons from the Moonlight Dance Studio."

Mel looked from her sister to the coupon then back to her sister. "What fresh hell is this?"

"Now hear me out, Mel. When you agreed to be maid of honor in my wedding you knew there would be certain expectations."

Melody stuck her hand on her hip. "Yes, wearing an ugly dress, throwing you a couple of parties and buying you a ridiculously-expensive gift. *Those* are the duties I've agreed to fulfill."

"A Keenan Okofi original is hardly ugly," Stephanie said with a huff.

Mel rolled her eyes, knowing better than to insult the designs of her sister's husband-to-be. He was swiftly becoming one of the hottest new names in fashion, or so Stephanie claimed.

"I'm sorry, but you know what I mean. I don't see where dance lessons fit into this whole deal."

"Mel, it's a formal candlelight wedding with a twelve-piece orchestra. There will be a lot of dancing, including the bridal party dance."

"I don't need lessons to rock and sway around the floor a few times with Keenan's sixteen-year-old brother."

"I'll have you know that Samir goes to boarding school in London where ballroom dance is a part of the daily curriculum."

"Poor kid," she scoffed.

"Mel, there will be a lot of important people there. Don't you want to make a good impression?"

Melody felt an icy tingle of suspicion at those words. They were all too familiar. "Did Mother put you up to this?"

Stephanie winced, dropping her gaze to the floor.

There wasn't any use in denying it, Melody thought. Their mother had never given up trying to mold her eldest daughter into the perfect image of African-American high society—no matter how futile the effort.

Stephanie reached out to squeeze Melody's arm. "Okay, she might have made the suggestion, but you know I *never* would have gone along with it if it hadn't been a good one. Our wedding guests aren't just important to me, but to Keenan's career as well. Some of them may ask you to dance, and I don't want you to feel uncomfortable."

"Oh, this is about *my* comfort? Because if it is…" She pointed to her red Converse All-Stars.

"Melody, please. It's just five lessons. They'll teach you three different styles of dance. Just enough to get you through the wedding reception. Say you'll do it…please, please, please?"

Melody sighed. She was the black sheep in her family of New York socialites—and she was proud of it. Left to her own devices, she would have loved to send a message to her mother: her eclectic lifestyle wasn't a phase, her friends weren't going to morph into well-placed celebrities, and she was never going to marry rich.

But, for a change, this wasn't between just Melody and her mother. She was close to her sisters—both Stephanie and their youngest sibling, Vicky. And she'd already promised to do whatever chores were necessary to make Stephanie's dream wedding a success. Apparently that included clopping around the dance floor like a horse in ballet slippers.

"You're lucky I love you, Steph, because I wouldn't risk this kind of humiliation for just anyone."

"Thank you, big sis," Stephanie screeched, crushing her in a tight hug. "Now wait until you see Keenan's latest designs for the bridesmaids' dresses. I've changed my mind about the black-and-white ball gowns. We're thinking of going with these authentic African robes in red and gold…."

* * *

Will Coleman glanced at his watch. It was time to start class and there was still one student on the roster who hadn't arrived. Someone always bailed at the last minute.

Rubbing his hands together, he moved to the center of the studio floor. "Good evening, everyone. This is Beginners Ballroom Dance, and I'm your instructor, Will. In this class you'll learn the fox-trot, swing and waltz. Are you ready to get started?"

The class mumbled a faint response. "Okay, I'd like everyone to line up across from their partners. Followers on the right, leaders on the left."

Will turned around to close the curtain that sectioned off the large dance floor, and a movement in the doorway caught his eye. A young woman was trying to sneak away.

"Excuse me for one second," he said to the class and walked over to poke his head into the hallway.

"Miss? Miss, are you looking for Beginners Ballroom Dance?"

The woman turned slowly, clearly embarrassed. For a second Will thought he might have made a mistake. This woman didn't look anything like his typical dance students.

She was dressed in tan cargo pants, low black boots and a scanty black tank top that revealed a tattoo of a Chinese character on the small of her back.

"Um, I didn't realize I needed a partner, so…" She shrugged and took a step backward, clutching the end of her long braid in her fist.

He motioned her forward. "You don't need a partner. Come on in."

She hovered in place, clearly unsure what to do. Will reached out and took her by the wrist, gently pulling her into the room. She came willingly at first, but began to resist when she saw the lineup of the class.

"Everyone's paired up already," she whispered to him.

Will smiled, trying to put her at ease. "Don't worry about that. We do a lot of rotating, but you can start out as my partner."

A look of pure horror contorted her face, and he laughed out loud. "Trust me," he said, leading her over to where the other ladies were already lined up. "This will be completely painless."

Will was intrigued with his new student, but all eyes were on him, waiting patiently for instruction, so he couldn't indulge his fascination with her.

"Today we're going to learn the fox-trot. This is one of the most common patterns associated with ballroom dancing. It's the one that Fred Astaire and Ginger Rogers made famous. The rhythm for the fox-trot is slow, slow, side step. Slow, slow, side step."

He demonstrated the steps first for the men and then for the women. "Okay, now has everyone got that?"

Across the room, he could already see that his pretty new student was having trouble. She was struggling to shift her weight and not trip on the side step.

"Let me emphasize for the ladies that you'll be stepping back with your right foot. So it's right, left, side step. Good, now let's partner up and give it a try."

He motioned for his reluctant partner to join him in the center of the room. "What's your name?"

"Mel…uh, short for Melody," she answered softly.

"Okay, class, Melody is going to help me demonstrate proper frame. Square up with your partner like this." Will explained the basics of frames and maintaining proper resistance between partners.

Normally, he could recite this spiel in his sleep, but today he was struggling to concentrate. There were too many variables splitting his attention. First, he had to keep his eye on the rest of the class to be sure they were keeping up. Next, he had to help his timid partner who was fighting him every step of the way. And finally, he was trying to keep his hands from sliding off her tiny top to her bare skin.

"Not so much resistance, Melody," he said to her, then louder to the class, "Followers should be pushing against the leader's shoulder *lightly*. Keep in mind we're dancing, not wrestling."

Melody wrinkled her nose. "Why do you keep calling us followers?"

At this proximity, Will was tempted to whisper his answer directly into her ear. Instead, he forced himself to remain in instructor mode. "Did you hear that, class? Melody would like to know why I keep referring to the ladies as followers. Anyone want to answer that question?"

A stocky young man with swarthy Italian features piped up, "Because the men are always in charge." A few of the women in the class groaned.

"That's right, on the dance floor, the men are always the leaders. It's the woman's job to receive signals from the man and follow through. Now let's try the step together."

Will continued to try and lead the class while dancing with Melody, but it was becoming obvious that she wasn't picking up the movements as quickly as the rest of the class. "Whoa, Melody, you don't move until I move."

She released an exasperated breath. "Then why bother teaching me the step at all if I'm not allowed to do it? I can be your little puppet, and you can move my legs for me."

Startled by her outburst, Will reminded himself that first-time dancers became frustrated easily. He tried to soothe her by speaking softly. "Learning to follow isn't easy. It's a skill, just like leading. You'll pick it up eventually."

A rumble of voices caught Will's attention, and he realized that he'd gotten so caught up in helping Melody that he'd neglected the rest of the class. He'd failed to stagger the couples at the start of the lesson, and now they'd danced themselves into a crowded jumble in one corner of the room.

"I'm sorry, class, this is my fault. Let me have three couples on the right side of the room and four on the left." Will left Melody to practice a few steps on her own as he made his rounds to the other couples. Then he led Melody to the center of the room once again.

"How are you doing? Think you've got it now?" He pulled her into position before she could respond. "Good, now let's try the patterns all together. Slow, slow, side step…slow, slow—don't step back so far, Melody, you're going to—"

Will tried to catch her, but it was too late. Melody's rubber-soled boots stopped short, but her body kept going and she slipped through his grasp. With a pathetic thud, she landed on her backside at his feet.

"Thank you, class. That will be all for today."

Chapter 2

The dance instructor offered a hand to help Melody to her feet, but she pushed him away and dragged herself up. "I've got it."

She spun around, making a beeline for the exit. Stephanie had wasted her money. Walking on hot coals carrying an anvil was time well spent compared to this.

"Hold on! Melody, wait." Will caught up with her and halted her with a hand on her shoulder. "Are you okay? Did you injure yourself?"

When she didn't immediately turn, he held her

shoulder firmly and spun her around. The bold, masculine move surprised her, and his touch shot through her like an electrical jolt. Heat rushed to her cheeks so quickly, they tingled. Melody jerked out of his grasp, annoyed at Will for having the nerve to reduce her to mush—and at herself for complying.

This wasn't right. She didn't get all gooey inside every time an attractive man looked her way. On the contrary, *she* was the one to turn men into jiggling mounds of jelly. They found *her* intimidating—as well they should.

She lifted her chin. "I'm fine. I'm perfectly fine."

"Please accept my apology. That spill you just took was entirely my fault."

"Damn, you're smooth," she whispered.

"What?"

Dear Lord, had she really just said that out loud? Just when she thought things couldn't possibly get worse… "I mean, how could my clumsiness be your fault? It's obvious that I don't belong here."

"Nonsense, it's my job to maintain the frame. I got distracted and let it go slack. That's why you fell."

Melody opened and closed her mouth. Was this guy for real? Nobody had *that* much class.

She'd grown up surrounded by the wealthy upper crust, and they were some of the most entitled, unapologetic types she'd known. But this guy was nothing like them—despite the fact that everything about him screamed money, from his diamond-studded watch to his designer slacks and silk crew-neck shirt.

Maybe he hadn't been born wealthy. That would explain it. On his hands, as well-manicured as they were, she'd felt a few masculine ridges that hinted at physical labor.

Nevertheless, he wasn't her type at all. Way too clean-cut. She was so over neatly-cropped hair and a clean shave. But when he smiled, his straight white teeth made a striking contrast against his deep brown skin. And his chocolate-brown eyes were filled with kindness. Her heart jumped in her chest.

This was getting too weird. Time to cut and run. "Look, this isn't working out, so I'm not going to waste any more of your time or mine."

His brow wrinkled. "Don't tell me you're not coming back."

She scoffed. "Oh, I'm telling *you* before you tell *me*."

"You can't give up. You just need to relax a little."

Mel rolled her eyes. "No, I was awful."

"It's only natural that you'd feel tense standing before the entire class. Believe me, you'd do much better with no one watching. Come here." Will held out his hand.

"Now?"

"Of course. I don't have any more classes this evening. I want you to see that you can learn to dance." He flicked the switch on the stereo remote, turning on the music. "Come here."

Reluctantly, Melody moved into his arms. He was right, it was a lot different without anyone watching…but not in the way that he'd meant.

Suddenly she noticed the intoxicating scent of his cologne. She saw his biceps bulging underneath his shirt. And she was very aware of the proximity of their bodies.

She was so overwhelmed by all these new sensations that she forgot her anxiety over dancing. Mel let herself be swept across the floor in his arms.

"That's it. See what a difference it makes when you relax and trust your partner?"

Melody looked down and lost her footing,

throwing them out of sync. She swore under her breath.

"It's okay, we'll pick it back up. Slow, slow, side step. Just follow me."

Melody tried to repeat the rhythm over and over in her head so as not to embarrass herself again. "I think I'm getting it."

"That's right. All you have to do is trust me. You don't even have to know the moves ahead of time. Watch." Will broke their frame and twirled her in a circle and turned her at an angle in several more complicated patterns.

Melody glided right along with him, wide-eyed that she was actually dancing. "I don't believe I did all that," she said when he resumed the basic pattern.

"Well, you did." He stopped. "Now that wasn't so bad, was it?"

She felt her skin flushing. She felt like a high-school girl. In fact, she couldn't remember the last time she'd felt this much like a girl of any sort. "It was okay," she said, trying to hide her giddiness.

"And next week will be even better. Promise me you'll come back?"

Melody looked up into those deep brown eyes and found herself saying the opposite of what she'd planned. "I promise."

* * *

Will regulated his breathing as he increased his pace on the treadmill. He felt his body kick into the zone as sweat began to bead on his forehead.

"Would you be interested in joining the activity-planning committee?" A petite woman wearing a hot-pink sports bra and designer shorts stepped in front of his treadmill.

Will tried to hide his frustration as he slowed his pace. "Excuse me?" he asked, panting.

The woman leaned forward, propping one arm on the electronic panel, inadvertently skewing his workout settings. "I know you're fairly new to Parkview Heights, and the best way to get to know your neighbors is to join the planning committee. I'm the chair, Abby Rutherford." She held out her hand.

Will was forced to stop the treadmill and step off. After first wiping his palm on his shorts, he reluctantly shook her hand. "Nice to meet you, Abby. I'm Will."

Bending over, hands on his knees, Will stared at the floor, trying to appear as though he were catching his breath. In reality he was reining in his temper.

"We meet the first Thursday of every month to

plan the following month's events. Can I sign you up for our next meeting in two weeks?"

Will started to answer but was interrupted when another woman sidled up beside Abby and gave her a one-armed hug. In her other arm, the woman carried a Chihuahua in a purple sweatband and Spandex tank that matched her own. They exchanged greetings and parted with air kisses.

"Don't forget *The Apprentice* viewing party in the club floor lounge next Monday," Abby tossed over her shoulder as the woman headed for the juice bar.

"Sorry about that," Abby said to Will. "As you can see, committee events are a big hit, and you'll get to meet all your neighbors." Her smile turned from friendly to flirtatious.

"Abby, I'd love to join your committee, but I'm afraid my work schedule is really hectic for the next few weeks."

Will had only been a resident of the luxury apartment complex for three weeks, so he *was* interested in meeting new people, but not in the middle of a workout.

He'd been varying his exercise routine in the penthouse health club hoping to avoid his chatty neighbors. It was quickly becoming apparent that Parkview residents didn't come to the gym to work out, they came to be seen.

On his first visit, he'd felt strangely under-dressed for the gym. He'd shown up in faded sweats and a paint-splattered T-shirt, while everyone else wore color-coordinated designer labels. He'd barely noticed anyone breaking a sweat. His own workout had progressed slowly because all the machines were tied up with men and women carrying on leisurely conversations while they kept up the vague appearance of exer-cising.

Cutting his losses, Will rode the elevator back down to his apartment. The thought of buying his own exercise equipment flashed in his mind for the umpteenth time, and for the umpteenth time he dismissed it.

Despite his hard-won status as one of New York's more successful stockbrokers, the lifestyle was still too new for him to abandon his working-class values. He just couldn't waste money on expensive workout machines when his exorbitant rent covered a fully-equipped gym just three floors up. And since he belonged to a rare group of individuals who actually took full advantage of the state-of-the-art machines, the equipment was in excellent condition.

Will dragged his towel across the back of his neck as he entered his apartment. Getting accepted by the Parkview Housing Committee had been an arduous seven-week process involving background checks, prying interviews and several reference letters from well-placed individuals. Now that he was here, the hassle had been worth it. The exclusive residence represented a lifelong climb from Brooklyn factory work to Wall Street success.

Of course things were different here. Different from working two jobs to get by. Different from backbreaking manual labor, sleep-deprivation and night school. Different had been exactly what Will was looking for.

It was just going to take some getting used to, that's all. But, in the meantime, he needed a dose of reality.

Will sat on the couch with his cordless phone and dialed his younger brother's number. Tony answered right away.

"Will! Hey, man, what's up? How's Park Avenue life treating you? No wait, don't tell me. I'm not in the mood to shoot myself."

Tony always pretended that he wanted to switch places with Will, but he knew his brother better than that. Tony had always been quite content with the cards life had dealt him. Will had been the dissatisfied one.

By contrast, Tony had always worked at the plastics factory and had never pursued another career path. He'd started a family at eighteen and was happy with the small apartment he lived in with his wife and three sons. Will knew this because once he'd begun making money, he'd offered to move them into a big house, or upgrade their ten-year-old car, and all of these offers had been firmly refused. Christmases and birthdays were the only occasions Will was allowed to spend money on them, and even then, extravagant gifts were returned.

"Everything's fine here." Will heard cheering in the background. "What's going on over there?"

"Oh, you know how we do. The boys are watching basketball. Frieda's making hot wings."

"I *love* Frieda's wings," Will said in an unmistakable plea for an invitation.

"Then come on over, man. You know you're always welcome here."

Will started to accept his brother's offer, but

Tony continued, "It's funny, when you moved to the other side of the tracks, I was worried we wouldn't see you much. But, you've been back in the 'hood almost every day. Basketball at the rec center, pizza night at Shucky's Bar, you even showed up for dominoes at Little Harold's two nights ago."

Will laughed sheepishly. "What are you trying to say? Are you getting tired of me?"

"Nah, bro, nothing like that. I'm just wondering why you worked so hard to get out of the 'hood, just so you could come back and hang here every other night. What's the matter? Park Avenue ain't all it's cracked up to be?"

"Of course it is," Will answered quickly. "It's great. Everything's great. Really great." *Stop saying* great, *you idiot!*

"Good. Don't forget I'm an old married man. I have to live through you. You're supposed to be dating some model chick and going to bougie parties where they serve snails and crap like that."

"Yeah, yeah, all that's on the agenda. I've just been…working a lot. I still teach dance two nights a week."

"You can't work all the time. What about dating? Meet any hot girls lately?"

"Hot girls?" A tattooed girl with combat boots and a waist-length braid flashed in his brain. "Oh yeah, they're everywhere."

"Ahhh, yeah! Talk to me."

"Actually, that's why I was calling. I wanted you and the kids to know you wouldn't be seeing me as much in the next few weeks. Between work, the dance studio and my impending social life, my schedule's starting to look pretty tight."

"Glad to hear it, man. The boys will miss seeing you around, but we'd all rather you had a life. I was starting to wonder if you were afraid to live in that crystal palace you worked so hard to get into."

Will felt heat wash down his neck as the truth of Tony's words hit home. "Wow, you suddenly getting deep on me, bro?"

"Hey, I gotta make sure you're all right. Park Avenue's a different world. All your peeps are still in Brooklyn."

"You have nothing to worry about. Everything is fine."

"Cool. Then the only other explanation is that you still haven't figured out how to work that talking stove of yours."

Will laughed hard into the phone, then paused. "How did you know?"

"All right, man, jump in the car and get over here before Frieda's wings get cold."

Melody waited in the corner of the dance studio as other couples began to arrive. As the trendy men and women around her chatted amongst themselves or practiced last week's lesson, Mel chided herself for coming back to class.

She didn't fit in here. Normally, that was a good thing. But today Mel felt dopey for showing up to class fifteen minutes early. It was silly to have sweaty palms and a stomach doing somersaults. And she felt extra foolish for wearing her black pleated mini skirt to impress the teacher.

She glanced down at the chunky sports watch on her wrist as she eyed the door. Three minutes to go. Maybe she could still—

"Good evening, class." Will Coleman walked into the room, eliminating all hope of a quick escape. "I'm glad to see some of you practicing."

Melody swallowed hard, hating the sudden giddiness she felt at the sight of him. He wore tan slacks with a fitted knit shirt that showed off his muscular build. His leather belt matched his brown loafers perfectly. He looked neat. Conservative. *Delicious*.

She blinked. What was getting into her? Since when was conservative delicious?

Feeling a tiny bit self-conscious, Mel glanced at her mirrored image on the opposite wall. He'd told them to wear leather-soled shoes. The only pair she owned were her black studded cowboy boots. With those she wore opaque gray tights and her mini skirt with black-and-white suspenders hanging free at her waist. On top she wore a black baby-T sporting the word *Brat* in angry white letters. To complete the look, she'd positioned two ponytails at the back of her head and then bound them together with randomly-spaced rubber bands in a variety of colors.

This was as dressed-up as she got. So he'd damn well better appreciate it.

Will caught her eye and gave her a warm smile. Her knees went weak. And weakness made Melody bitter. She lifted her chin, finding composure in defiance.

"Okay, class, let's line up. Followers on the right. Leaders on the left."

Melody got in line. The numbers were still uneven. Will would have to be her partner again. Her heart began to race.

"Now that you all know the basic steps, I want

you to get a feel for dancing with different partners. Start with the person directly across from
you, and after a few minutes, we'll rotate."

Melody's heart sank. She was anxious to show
Will how much she'd improved. At least she'd get
to dance with the teacher first, she thought as he
approached her.

"Melody, do you mind practicing on your own
for this round? I need to be mobile to monitor
everyone's progress," he said quietly to her, and
then more loudly, "Class, each follower will have
to dance one round on their own. But don't worry,
we'll keep rotating so everyone will have a
partner most of the time."

It was all Mel could do not to groan out loud.
Why on earth had she come back? Trying not to
embarrass herself, Melody dutifully ran through
the steps on her own and was feeling pretty confident when it was time to rotate.

An older man with silver hair and a friendly
smile walked up to her. He extended his hand.
"Hi, my name is George."

"I'm Mel, um, Melody."

"Pleasure to meet you, Melody." George took
her into his arms. The music started and he glided
with her around the floor with expertise.

"Are you sure you need lessons?" she asked her partner.

"This is more of a refresher course for me. My wife Gretchen is the one who really wants to learn."

Melody was disappointed when it was time to rotate. It had been nice to dance with someone who knew what he was doing but didn't stir up those pesky butterflies.

Her next partner, Scott, was a bit more of a challenge. Clearly nervous, he stayed two beats ahead of the music. Feeling good about her progress, Mel took the lead and Scott let her.

"You're a great dancer," the redhead said and his face flushed as he struggled not to meet her eyes.

"Thank you."

Scott moved on quickly, catching sight of the reproachful looks his girlfriend was shooting from across the room.

Her next partner appeared before her, the stocky Italian she remembered from the previous week. "Hi, I'm Melody."

"Joey," he said curtly and jerked her into position.

His grip was tight and Melody constantly felt

off balance. She tried pushing against him to get control of her footing.

Joey clamped her into a firmer grip and physically moved her across the floor.

"Dude, loosen up." She pushed against him harder.

"Hey, stop trying to lead."

"Fine, but you need to stop trying to bulldoze me."

The two of them moved awkwardly across the floor, occasionally creating so much resistance in their frame that they looked like wrestlers battling for a title belt.

When Joey missed a beat, Mel would try to force him to catch up. "Quit leading," Joey muttered.

"You're off beat."

"You're supposed to follow me, no matter what." He applied more force to their frame.

Feeling red-hot anger creeping up her spine, Melody applied some force of her own. "It would help if you were doing it right."

They were so caught up in their power struggle that neither of them noticed that the music had stopped and the entire class was watching them.

Will walked over. "What's the problem?"

"She won't quit leading," Joey piped up like the whiney tattletale he was.

Mel took a deep breath, trying not to show Will just how evil her temper could get. "I wasn't trying to lead," she bit out. "I was just trying to keep him from sweeping the floor with my heels."

"She's some kind of control freak."

Melody whirled on Joey, but before she could even think of wrapping her fingers around the man's neck, Will had pulled her into his arms. Lifting her arm over her head, he spun her back around in a graceful twirl.

"Okay, class, that's enough rotating for today. Go back to your original partners. We're going to learn some turns."

Chapter 3

For the remainder of class, Will kept Melody at his side as he showed them how to add spins to the basic patterns they'd learned. Once again, as he was dismissing the students and giving them instructions on what to practice for next week, Melody tried to slip out.

"You're trying to sneak off again?" Will called out before she reached the door.

She turned to face him, looking sheepish.

"I'm going to start taking it personally."

She walked back over to him. "I just don't

think I have the right temperament for ballroom dancing. I'm not a let-a-guy-control-me type of girl."

Will let his gaze travel over Melody. She'd struck a brazen pose, hip jutted out and arms crossed. Her catlike eyes, ringed with dark liner, dared him to contradict her. No, she wasn't the passive type.

Speaking of types. She wasn't his at all. Her fashion sense was a mix of goth and grunge instead of Gaultier and Gucci. Melody Rush was dark, defiant and every bit the brat her shirt proclaimed.

He took in the shapely legs stemming from her low black cowboy boots and the rippled abs peeking out of her baby-T. On the other hand, she was *sexy* and he was a man. It just didn't go much deeper than that.

"Melody, you've got it all wrong. Just because the man leads doesn't mean the woman is passive. It's our job to make *you* look good. Like the pedestal under a Ming vase—the man bears the weight so the woman can be admired."

"Yeah, that's cute, but you can't tell me after today that I'm cut out for this. Dancing with some of the guys was okay, but that last one—" Melody formed her hands into a choking gesture.

Will stifled a smirk. "It takes a while to adjust to new partners. The more confident you become in your own dancing ability, the easier it will be for you to adapt to a new partner's style."

"You make it sound so easy, but I'm not buying it. I've barely gotten used to *this* pattern, and now you're talking about teaching swing next week? That's the one where they throw you around like a rag doll, right?"

"That's one way to look at it," Will said, amused. "If it will make you feel better, I'll give you a sneak peek at next week's lesson. That way you can practice a few steps on your own."

Suddenly Melody looked nervous. "No, I don't want to waste your time. The studio's closing. You probably want to get home."

He took a step toward her, holding out his hand. "It's no problem."

She took a step back, and he paused. "Unless you'd rather not." He liked the fact that he could rattle her. He could tell that was something that didn't happen often.

She visibly swallowed and took his hand. "Hey, if you're up for it, I am, too. I guess I need all the help I can get."

Taking the stereo remote from his pocket, he

hit the CD changer and a bouncy swing filled the room. "Okay, the basic swing pattern is relatively simple—one, two, rock step."

He had to show her several times before the rock step began to sink in. "Loosen up. You've got to let yourself *feel* the connection. Try not to think so hard."

Melody stumbled. "I don't know about this. Swing seems so corny."

"Corny? The swing? No way. It's the most versatile dance of them all. I bet you didn't know that you can swing to hip-hop music." He pulled the remote from his pocket and the CD switched to a pounding beat. Will continued to lead her through the basic pattern.

Melody wrinkled her nose. "Hip-hop isn't exactly my thing."

He twirled her around then spun her around his back. "Oh that's right, goth girls are more into metal, right?"

"I'm not much for labels, but yeah, I like rock, punk, alternative…"

"Hmm, I've never tried to swing to punk music before. Maybe if you bring some in, we could try it out."

She regarded him with a wary eye. "Maybe."

"There you go." He led her around the room. "You're getting the hang of it now."

He watched Melody trying to fight back her grin. "It's all right, I guess," she said.

Feeling her confidence growing, Will led her into more complicated steps. Melody followed along like a pro.

"I have to know, what made you want to take ballroom-dancing lessons?" he asked, pulling her close.

Melody scoffed. "Do I look like someone who would *want* ballroom-dancing lessons? No, I'm the maid of honor in my sister's circus—I mean *wedding*. I think she only gave me the title in order to inflict girly tortures upon me—ballroom dancing, pointy-toed shoes, hot rollers…"

The image of Melody in pink taffeta and ruffles scowling at her sister from the front of a church sent a rush of laughter up from his diaphragm. He missed a beat, throwing them off for a second. "Come on, it isn't that bad, is it?"

"Oh, it's going to be bad. My family gets one favor and this is it. I only have to be presentable for a few hours," she muttered through clenched teeth.

Will laughed. "Well, don't worry about a thing. I'll make sure you're the belle of the ball."

Right on queue, Melody faltered. "I'll settle for not falling on my butt."

"No problem." He lowered her into a steep dip so that she was barely skimming the floor, then he whisked her up into a graceful turn.

His hands slid inside her T-shirt onto the smooth skin of her back. The song on the stereo had moved on to a pulsing erotic beat. For a brief second their eyes locked.

Melody immediately looked away. "So what's a nice guy like you doing in a place like this?" she asked when she'd regained her breath.

Will exhaled slowly, taking hold of her hands for less intimate contact.

"I'm a stockbroker. I teach dance part-time. It was one of many odd jobs I used to do, and I still love it."

"I figured it was a side job. Most people can't buy designer shoes and diamond watches on a teaching salary."

"I teach to stay sane. The stock market can be stressful. Dancing relaxes me."

"Dancing has the opposite effect on me, but I guess that stands to reason since I have two left feet."

"Nonsense, you're doing well." He took her

through another pattern. "See that? You've just learned two weeks worth of steps in fifteen minutes. Next week, you'll be way ahead of the class."

"Great, now I've probably forgotten everything I learned from the last two weeks."

"Not a chance. I'll show you." Will changed the music to a romantic melody by Frank Sinatra. He took her into his arms and the two of them immediately fell into fox-trot step.

Will had danced with many women. Old, young, the talented, the uncoordinated and some of the most beautiful, graceful dancers in New York. But there was something he just loved about dancing with Melody.

Dancing with her awakened primitive responses in him he'd never felt before. She would hate to know it but *because* she was so resistant to being controlled, making her body bend to his will gave him a rush of power.

She had the body of a ballerina, and all the grace of an elephant. But, he was skilled enough to compensate for that. He turned her this way and that, watching her hips and arms move in perfect concert with his. He didn't want to take his hands off of her.

Will thought she'd been enjoying it, too, until she suddenly jerked out of his arms and pushed him away. She'd moved so quickly he stumbled back a few steps before catching himself.

"I'm sorry. I'm sorry—I think I've got it now."

Will stared at her, still stunned by her sudden retreat. "Um, okay…"

"Sorry, I didn't mean to—it's just that it's getting late. I think I should go."

He nodded. "Okay."

"I mean, thank you—for this. I think it really helped."

She was chattering a mile a minute. And the truth began to sink into Will's head. She didn't know how to handle the attraction between them. He had two choices. He could be professional: slow down, put her at ease and make her feel safe, or…

"I understand. All of this can get overwhelming. Maybe it would help you to get out onto a real dance floor. The Franklin Hotel has cocktails and dancing every Monday night. I could take you after class next week. You'll have the chance to practice in a less structured environment."

From the look of pure dread in her eyes, Will was certain Melody would turn him down.

"Next week?" Her voice squeaked slightly.

"Yes."

Her brow furrowed. "After class?"

"Yes."

"Just the two of us?"

Will nodded. "That's right."

He watched her swallow.

"Okay."

Melody breathed a sigh of relief as she stepped into the familiar territory of Alchemy that night—on Mondays it was goth night. There was something so comforting about the red neon skull glowing in the window after an evening in that highbrow dance studio.

Stage lights washed the normally stark walls in a hazy red, and a blue spotlight swirled around the three-man band raging on the tiny stage. Off to one side of the cramped room akin to someone's basement apartment, she found her friends at a table far from the stage.

"There she is. Finished with ballet class?" Bass called to her.

Mel rolled her eyes. "It's not ballet—it's ballroom dancing. And it figures you wouldn't know the difference." She pulled up a chair.

"Ballet or ballroom…either way, I've just got to see this. Aren't you going to show us what you've learned?" asked her friend, Roland.

People at Alchemy didn't dance so much as let the music vibrate through them into pulsating—almost convulsive—rocking motions.

"Only if you're my partner. Do you think you're up for it, Roland?" Mel challenged.

Roland, with his pale skin and thick, black-framed glasses could easily be mistaken for a college professor. He wore slim black pants, and a black V-neck sweater with a white T-shirt. In fact, he'd look better suited for a library than Alchemy if it weren't for the spiky black hair that jutted in sharp angles from the top of his head…and the red lipstick.

Roland glanced at his girlfriend Samantha, whom they all affectionately referred to as Tha. "How about it, Tha? Do you dare me?"

Tha was a bleached blonde with three inches of black roots. She wore lip and eyebrow piercings and heavy metallic-green eye shadow. She just shrugged without looking up from her beer. "Mel's going to make you look like a dork. But, if you're cool with that, then I'm cool with it."

Roland got up and moved into an empty space at the back of the bar. Mel shook her head as she followed him. Punk music blared from the speakers above her head. Counting quickly, she abandoned any thoughts of a fox-trot.

"Normally, the man leads. But, between the two of us, I think I qualify the most." She took Roland's hands and showed him the pattern Will had taught her earlier that evening. "One, two, rock step. Got it?"

Roland looked baffled.

The beat of the music was frantic, but they eventually managed to fall into a crazed, but steady rhythm. They were doing well enough that Bass and Tha soon joined them, frantically trying to imitate their movements. After several minutes, other people in the club got up to join them.

The band, energized by the dancing crowd, played two extra songs before ending their set for a break. Mel and her friends returned to their table out of breath.

"I can't wait to tell Will you really can swing dance to punk music," Mel said to herself.

Just then, a man Melody had never seen before set a beer down in front of her. "You looked like you could use a drink," he said with a flirtatious smile.

Melody looked from the drink to the guy, then back at the drink.

"What's the matter, don't you drink?" he asked.

Mel picked up the glass and passed it back to him. "I don't drink anything *you* bring me."

The guy stood staring blankly for a moment before finally wandering off.

Samantha shook her head at her. "You never cease to amaze me. Everywhere we go, men fall all over themselves trying to impress you. You always shoot them down without batting an eyelash."

Melody shrugged. "I didn't ask him for the drink. He volunteered for bartending duty."

"One of these days you're going to run into a guy who's not scared of you."

Mel shook her head, folding her arms across her chest. "It'll never happen," she said, more confidently than she felt.

Deep down, she knew she may have already met that man.

Chapter 4

"Funny, but you don't strike me as the wall-flower type."

Will snapped out of his reverie to find himself the target of an unabashed feminine once-over. Standing only five foot five in her glittering three-inch pink pumps, his appraiser craned her neck to take in his full length.

Parkview's club floor lounge was teeming with trendy singles that Friday night, but all Will could think about was the Knicks game he was missing. His new wide-screen TV had been delivered earlier that week. At that moment, he should have been watching the Knicks clobber the Bulls in high definition.

Abby, the planning-committee chair—hopped-up on a latte—had cornered him at the gym again this morning. She wouldn't let him get back to the stair-climber until he'd agreed to attend the mixer.

"Wallflower." The word tasted flat in his mouth. "Is that what I am?" he asked the beautiful young woman.

"You've been nursing that same drink since you got here, and you're holding up this wall as though the roof were caving in. So, yes, you're behaving like a wallflower." She sipped from the flared lip of her Cosmopolitan glass. "Is that really how you planned to spend this evening?" she asked with a sidelong glance.

He'd *planned* to spend the evening with the Knicks, but it was too late for that now. In that instant, Will made up his mind to make the best of the situation. His brother had been right—he needed to start living the lifestyle he'd worked so hard to afford.

He followed his new friend to the bar where he discovered her name was Valencia. As he bought her Cosmopolitans, she regaled him with her escapades as an interior designer for several big-name celebrities. He listened, smiled, flirted mildly and even took her number when she offered it.

As Will rode the elevator down to his apartment, he couldn't ignore the nagging feeling growing in the pit of his stomach.

He tried to brush the feeling away as he entered his apartment. Valencia was just what he needed right when he needed it—a professional woman who shared his tastes and desires. She was beautiful and petite with smooth dark skin and a trendy haircut. Just his type.

So why did he feel so…disinterested?

Dropping Valencia's card on the coffee table, Will grabbed his remote. There was still time to catch the end of the game. He stared blindly at the screen until his gaze drifted back to the phone number scrawled across the top of the card. On some strange level he felt as though he should have been with Melody.

But that was ridiculous. He hadn't done anything wrong. They weren't even dating. *Yet,* his mind finished silently.

Did taking her out for an extended dance lesson qualify as a date?

Will wasn't sure, but it surprised him how much he was looking forward to finding out.

Melody threw down her pencil in frustration and pushed away from her art board. She was supposed to be finishing the panels that introduced the Ambassador story line. Instead she kept absently sketching the angles in Will Coleman's face.

His face was handsome in all the conventional ways, but that wasn't what stirred her artist's fascination. It was the war going on behind his eyes.

He had the makings of a comic-book hero—boy-next-door good looks with a little something extra. The hint of a secret identity, maybe? With her pencil, she darkened his brow into a brooding look. The eyes always showed the strain of a double life.

Snatching the sketches of Will from her drawing board, she shoved them into a drawer. She was projecting qualities on to him that didn't exist. Will wasn't a superhero—no matter how perfect she made him out to be.

And she didn't have time to waste inventing new comic-book characters. She'd gotten up early that morning to get some work done before her house became overrun with wedding paraphernalia. Stephanie had begged her to let them use her apartment to address wedding invitations.

Melody had just started to get a rough outline of the Ambassador's first panel when she heard the doorbell ring.

Her heartbeat sped up as she crossed the room to get the door. "Bass," she said, feeling both relief and disappointment. "What are you doing here? My sister will be here any minute with her bridesmaids."

Bass leaned against the doorjamb, clutching his skateboard and a bag from CompuCity. "And good morning to you, too. I stopped by to check out the first draft of the Ambassador sketches. You said they'd be done this weekend."

Embarrassed at her lack of progress, Melody continued to block the entrance. "Since when do you get out of bed before noon on a Saturday?"

"It was an emergency. My motherboard blew up right in the middle of a Web site redesign." Bass looked over his shoulder to survey the empty hallway. "So what brings Bridezilla and her merry minions to your humble abode?"

"Stephanie's apartment is being painted and my mother—the etiquette Nazi—claims the Rush name will be dead in New York if we don't mail the invitations Monday. So you stand at the gateway to wedding hell."

"What about one of the other bridesmaids? Don't *they* have apartments?"

"I'm the maid of honor." She hung her head in mock sorrow. "It's my cross to bear."

"Well, this won't take long." He tried to look past her into the loft. "Show me the sketches and I'll be out of here before they arrive."

"Actually…" She grabbed his arm, pulled him into the room and slammed the door behind him. "Now that you're here, you should stick around and keep me sane. In a few minutes this place will be filled to the rafters with fancy stationery and ribbons."

Bass stumbled backward into the closed door. "Thanks, but I think I'd rather get a root canal from my blind uncle Harry."

Before Melody could respond, the doorbell rang again. "Too late. They're here and you can't escape."

"No way, you couldn't pay me—"

Melody opened the door and Bass lost the ability to speak. Two statuesque models preceded Stephanie into the apartment. He promptly flopped onto the sofa and crossed his ankles on the black trunk used as a coffee table.

"Where should I put these?" Stephanie huffed as she held out two large shopping bags filled with boxes.

"Over there." Mel pointed to the large wooden craft table that doubled as her dining table. The varnish was long gone and it was stained, paint-splattered and grooved, but she loved it more with each new flaw.

Melody was about to shut the door when she heard the elevator yawn open at the end of the hall. Out of habit, she stuck her head out to see who'd gotten off. Her breath caught. It took all her strength not to jump back into her apartment and slam the door.

Swallowing, Melody wiggled her fingers in a halfhearted wave and turned to her sister with gritted teeth. "You did *not* tell me Mother was coming to this thing."

Her sister at least had the decency to look embarrassed. "I didn't? I thought you knew she was bringing Vicky."

Dutifully, Melody waited by the door to greet her mother who flung her arms wide and brushed right past her. "There's the bride," she cried as she flitted across the room to envelop Stephanie.

Mel's gaze connected with her youngest sister

Vicky's. They both rolled their eyes and shared a private smile. Reaching out, Melody wrapped an arm around her sister's neck and tugged her into a tight hug.

At seventeen, Vicky was turning into a real beauty. She'd recently decided that she wanted to grow her hair to her waist like Melody's. It currently hung just past her shoulders, and Mel was certain her baby sister would tire of the idea before it could get as far as her back.

Vicky was heavily influenced by both of her older sisters—a bit of a tomboy like Mel, with a knack for shopping like Stephanie. And, of course, she carried the full weight of their mother's expectations on her shoulders.

All Rush women had been groomed to be role models in the African-American community. Beverly Rush presided over any and every minority-related organization or charity in the tri-state area. For her, image was everything, and today was no exception. She was the picture of elegance in her pearl-gray pantsuit, which perfectly complemented the silvery strands in her stylish bob.

Later, as the girls were all perched around Mel's big art table addressing envelopes by hand because her sister insisted on the "personal" touch, Melody knew this was one area in which she excelled.

Having paid her dues hand-lettering comic books, Mel was confident her penmanship was beyond reproach. She addressed her first envelope in calligraphy, underscoring the last line with an elegant flourish. "How's that, Stephanie?"

"Oh, Melody, that's fabulous. If we didn't have nearly five hundred to do, I'd ask you to do all the invitations. Doesn't that look great, Mother?"

Melody winced instinctively, but couldn't resist sliding her gaze in her mother's direction. Beverly Rush got up and circled the table to stand behind her—Mel presumed to study the envelope up close.

Instead, Beverly grabbed a handful of Melody's ponytail and wrapped it around her hand. "You *are* going to cut this for the wedding, aren't you? It would take Francisco hours to force all that hair into a bun. You don't want to take time away from the bride on her wedding day."

Vicky gasped and Stephanie shouted, "Mother, stop it! I'd rather die than ask Mel to cut her hair for my wedding."

Her mother released Melody's hair and

returned to her seat. "Well, Francisco is a genius. I'm sure he'll think of something."

Melody gripped the edge of the table. Two more months. She only had to endure this for *two more months*.

Bass came from the kitchen with the hors d'oeuvres she'd prepared. He passed finger sandwiches like a white-gloved waiter instead of a Web designer wearing black fingernail polish. He lingered beside Lana, the Nordic blonde, who took two sandwiches, much to everyone's surprise.

Melody suspected that Lana had a crush on Bass despite the disapproval of the other model, Jessica. Earlier she'd heard Lana remark to Jess that Bass resembled rocker Dave Navarro.

Beverly picked up a sandwich and sniffed it. Sensing the forthcoming snide remark, Melody cried out, "Don't eat them, Mother. They're loaded with carbs."

Both models dropped the sandwiches like poison. "They're not low-carb?"

As Will guided Melody into the Franklin Hotel, he wasn't sure what to expect. Melody Rush was proving to be anything but predictable.

Part of him had thought she would show up in army boots and a black shroud. Instead, she came to class in a brown broomstick skirt, black silk peasant blouse and slinky gold sandals. Her long tresses had been braided into three sections and then wrapped into a knot on top of her head.

She didn't exactly blend in, but a sore thumb she wasn't. It wasn't her attire, but her mood that was most surprising. In the short time he'd known her, he'd never seen Melody so quiet. This entire evening had probably been a mistake. What had he been thinking bringing Melody so far out of her element?

"Are you okay?" he asked as they rode the elevator down to the ballroom. "You've been quiet ever since we got into the cab. If you're not up for this, we can—"

"No, I'm fine. I'm sure this will be fine."

But, to Will, she looked anything *but* fine.

They entered the ballroom where it was already starting to get crowded. Several couples glided around the room as the live band played a waltz.

Fearing that Melody would panic and bolt, Will kept his hand firmly on her back. The trouble was, the feel of her back, warm to his touch through the thin silk of her top had him wishing they were in a room that wasn't quite so public.

They found an empty table and Will pulled out her chair. "The buffet is open. Do you want to eat or get a drink before we start dancing?"

"Actually, I think I'd just like to sit here and watch for a few minutes," she answered.

As they sat in silence, Will tried to take in their surroundings through Melody's eyes. It was a lavish ballroom decorated in lush fabrics of red and gold with ornate crystal chandeliers—she probably found it pretentious. The band wasn't bad, but they would only be playing classical pieces and old standards—no doubt boring for her. The couples on the dance floor displayed varying degrees of dance experience, but they were mostly older—no one Melody could relate to.

Will shook his head. Boring, stuffy and pretentious. This had definitely been a mistake.

As soon as the thought crossed his mind, Melody surprised him by breaking the silence. "Wow, this place is pretty nice."

His brows rose. "Really? You think it's nice? I was pretty convinced you were hating it. I'm sure this isn't the type of place you normally hang out."

She cocked her head. "To tell you the truth, it brings back memories. I wish I had a nickel for all the affairs not unlike this one my parents dragged me to in the past."

"Are you serious?" he asked, confused.

"My father's a politician. And my mother takes her role as a politician's wife very seriously— image is everything. 'The Rushes are role models to the rest of the African-American community.' That meant up until I was eighteen, I had to attend all the important social affairs with the family. Can you believe when I was sixteen my mother even made me have a cotillion?"

Will stared at Melody as though he were seeing her for the first time. "Wow. I had no idea. I never would have guessed…"

She stared down at her hands. "I know. To my mother's great chagrin, I don't reflect the image of my fine upbringing."

Will could hear the pain underlying words that were meant to be flippant.

"Thankfully, my mother was blessed with my two younger sisters who will walk in her footsteps. Stephanie especially. She's a fashion model who's marrying one of the last straight clothing designers in New York. Mother couldn't be more proud."

"I'm sure she's proud of you, too." At that moment, Will realized he had no idea what Melody Rush even did for a living. Luckily, she filled in the blank before he could ask.

"Proud of me? *Please.* I write comic books for a living. Combine that with the fact that I—these are her words—dress like a subway transient, and it should be clear. Yeah, my mother's approval is something I gave up on long ago."

Will studied Melody, wishing he could believe her. No matter what she said, he knew it had to be hard not be accepted for who she was.

"I used to be a big fan of comics when I was a kid," he said. "Which ones do you work on?"

"I launched the Delilah series. She's a—"

"Kick-ass sister in a yellow catsuit who electrocutes her enemies."

Melody's eyes lit up. "You've heard of her?"

"Yeah, I've seen my nephews reading Delilah comics many times. Wait until they find out that I know the creator of the series. This is amazing."

"Thanks," she said, clearly unflattered.

"Wait a minute. You're a woman under thirty with her own comic-book series? That's huge. You can't tell me your parents aren't impressed with that kind of success."

"Believe me, that kind of 'success' isn't even on their radar." Melody sighed. "That doesn't mean my mother's given up hope for me though. She still tries to mold me into her image of perfection. It's by virtue of that fact that I had something suitable to wear tonight."

"What do you mean?"

"For birthdays and Christmases my sisters get stereos and DVDs—I get clothes, makeup and salon appointments. This skirt and blouse are some of the few pieces that hadn't made it into the Goodwill bin yet. And these shoes are the bridesmaid shoes my mother's been pestering me to break in."

Will smiled at her. "Well, you look very nice. But, you'd look good in anything. You could have worn whatever made you feel comfortable. There's no one here you need to impress."

She stared at him for a long time before finally giving him a soft thank-you.

Feeling bad for making the situation awkward, Will gestured to the dance floor. "Are you ready?"

Melody popped up out of her chair. "I think I'll visit the ladies' room first."

Will had to resist the urge to follow her. He had no gauge of where her mood was now. He could only pray she wouldn't leap out of the bathroom window and ditch him.

Melody stared at her pasty face in the bath-room mirror. Will's unconditional acceptance had thrown her off guard. She'd started off the evening in a funk. She'd let her mother get to her, and now she didn't even know why.

Before dance class that evening, her mother had called to discuss Stephanie's bridal shower. The woman had made it clear that if Mel's plans weren't up to her standards she would be taking over. Since she had no plans to speak of, her mother began barking orders until Mel had a split-ting headache.

Thinking about it now made her angry. Splashing cold water on her face, Melody pushed her mother out of her mind. Her mother wasn't here now, and after the strange way she'd been acting all night, she wouldn't be at all sur-prised if Will thought she was climbing out of the bathroom window right now. No doubt he re-gretted bringing her.

Her chin lifted as she studied her reflection. This outfit wasn't her style, it was her mother's style. And Will said he wanted her to be comfortable.

She'd made up her mind. She was going to face this situation the way she faced everything. As herself.

Twisting her hair out of its knot, she pried open the braids until her hair streamed down to her waist in a wild spiraling mass.

She took out her dark liner pencil and ringed her eyes to chase off the tasteful conservative look she'd arrived with. Hot-red lips completed her face.

Now for the rest of her outfit. She looked down at her clothes. Rolling her eyes, Mel tore off the blouse revealing the black camisole beneath it.

"That's better," she said aloud, happy with the way the top gave the flowing skirt a bit of an edge. On impulse she thrust the blouse under the running faucet. Wringing and twisting it, she formed the blouse into a rope that she secured with rubber bands.

She used the rope to pull her long thick tresses into a high ponytail. Tucking in the edges of the rope, she was satisfied with her look. Much more herself.

She had planned to break in her bridesmaid shoes, but the gold sandals were already severely pinching her toes. She'd never get through even one dance with those things on.

As Melody was preparing to leave, a young woman entered the bathroom. "Is your name Melody?"

"Yes, that's me."

"Well, there's a guy outside looking for you. He wanted me to make sure you didn't climb out a window or something."

Chapter 5

Will paced back and forth in the narrow hallway in front of the restrooms. Logically, he knew Melody couldn't have *really* climbed out of the window. But, she could have slipped onto the elevator and taken a cab home.

"Looking for me?"

Relief washed over him at the sound of her voice, and he turned immediately to face her. He paused for several seconds trying to take in her unexpected transformation. "Melody?"

"Sorry I was gone for so long. I decided that

my outfit needed a few adjustments." She twirled around. "What do you think?"

With her dark-lined eyes and her hair spilling like black rivulets of lava from a peak at her crown, she looked like a jungle priestess. His eyes slid down over her filmy lingerie top, which revealed just the right amount of her cleavage, to her stockinged feet.

A grin curved his lips. "Honestly, you look great. Definitely more like yourself."

"Good," she said, linking her arm through his. "Then let's dance."

They dropped her shoes off at their table and then Will guided her onto the dance floor. "Are you sure you don't want to wear your shoes? I'd hate to step on your toes."

Melody laughed. "As if you could. You're way too smooth for that. Besides, I was more likely to break an ankle wearing those things. I don't know what the hell my sister was thinking when she picked those things out."

Will laughed, looking back at them. "Actually, with those spiky heels, they'd probably make better weapons than footwear." He led her into a slow fox-trot.

"That's right, and if Stephanie isn't careful I'm

going to use those shoes on her. She keeps changing her mind about what kind of dresses we'll be wearing. Since her fiancé is the designer, she thinks it's okay for her to keep changing her mind. We went from Cinderella-style ball gowns to African robes to tight sheaths with trains."

Will laughed. He was glad Melody was talking because he was finding himself more and more distracted. Even though he could feel the eyes of the other couples on them, he didn't care. He definitely felt like he was with the most interesting woman in the room.

Will guided Melody around the dance floor through two fox-trots, a waltz and a mambo. "Are you getting tired? Do you want to take a break?"

Melody glanced around the room and a sense of weariness crept up the back of Will's neck as she answered, "Yeah, I think we could use a break."

He headed back toward their table but was surprised to find that Melody wasn't following him. Glancing over his shoulder, he saw her making her way to the bandstand.

"What could she possibly—"

Will saw her take something out of her purse and hand it to the band leader. Seconds later, the band announced they were going on a break and raucous punk music filled the ballroom.

Melody skipped across the floor and grabbed his hand. "I wanted to show you something."

Still baffled, Will had no choice but to let himself be led onto the dance floor, which was conspicuously empty for the first time that night. Couples were clustered around the floor, their mouths agape with horror at the frenetic beat of the music.

Melody grabbed his hands and began a hurried version of the swing step he'd taught her. Will, still locked in a haze of confusion, was barely able to keep up. Staring down at her feet, he was mesmerized by her movements but helpless to imitate them due to the swirl of questions circling in his mind.

"How much did you have to pay that band leader to play this CD?"

"A hundred bucks."

"What!"

"Hey, I know a lot of musicians—even the fancy ones that play in joints like this are starving."

"Are you kidding me? That guy was willing to risk being banned from this venue for a hundred bucks? And you were willing to spend—"

"Shhh. Concentrate. You're not paying attention. One, two, rock step, one, two, rock step, one, two, rock step," she counted aloud for him.

Realizing that he was making a fool of himself regardless, Will gave in and fell into step with her. Strangely enough, he began to feel the rhythm of the pattern and took over the lead.

He began to lead her into new patterns she hadn't learned before, but she followed him naturally. They laughed at how their old dance pattern fell in step with this frantic music.

Will was having such a good time, he barely noticed that the other dancers had joined them on the floor. The couples crowded around them, watching their movements and quickly matching the familiar swing steps to their rhythm.

As that song ended and a new punk song rocked through the ballroom, Will watched a Franklin Hotel manager standing in the doorway laughing his head off at the sight of New York's polished ballroom dancers swing-dancing to a song called "Purgatory."

By the time they finally cleared the dance floor for a much-needed break, the free buffet had been cleared away, and the bartender was already offering a last call.

Will smiled over at Melody as he summoned a cab. "You know, you're a fun date."

She threw him a sidelong glance. "Oh, is this a date? I hope you don't expect me to put out when you didn't even buy me dinner."

Will instructed the class to repeat their last pattern as he ducked into the hallway. He was entirely too distracted today, and he had to pull it together. He didn't know if it was a good or a bad thing that next week would be their last class. He enjoyed teaching Melody, but it was having a noticeable effect on the rest of the class.

In addition to the verbal blunders that had been tripping off his tongue all evening, he'd put the wrong music on the stereo twice. And Melody seemed to be enjoying his discomfort through all of this.

He knew she liked to watch him squirm. That had to be the reason she'd floored him with that sassy remark about him not having bought her dinner last week.

While he'd stared back at her, as white as a sheet, she'd claimed she was kidding and punched him in the arm. Of course he'd known she was kidding. But that did nothing for the images that had been haunting him ever since she'd uttered that anything-but-innocent remark.

"Are you okay?" Melody called out to him from the doorway.

Will deliberately took a sip from the water fountain before answering her. "I'm fine. Why aren't you inside practicing with the others?"

"Come on, there's only so much spinning around in a circle I can do by myself without feeling like a moron. You're supposed to be my partner."

"Melody, I don't want anyone in class to get the wrong idea about us—"

Melody tossed her head back and laughed. "Too late for that. They've already got ideas, and I'm not so certain they're the wrong ones."

"What are you talking about?"

"I got to class early and heard the McFeeneys speculating on whether or not there's something going on between the two of us."

He felt the blood drain from his face. "Are you serious?"

"Relax. You know, it's pretty obvious to every-one that you have a thing for me. Even before your absentminded-professor routine today."

Will shook his head in resignation. "Is that so?"

"Yes, so you may as well give in. I promise not to break your heart."

"Oh? And how do you know I won't break yours?"

Her chin lifted defiantly. "You break my heart and I'll break your nose," she said, shaking her fist at him.

Her tone was joking yet Will didn't doubt her seriousness for a moment.

"Get back to class," he said, facing the water fountain. "I'll be there in a minute."

After dance class, Melody hung around as she usually did. Which was probably the reason the class had begun speculating that they had something going on. They had no formal plans to meet for extra lessons this evening, but after their so-called date, it was clear to Melody that Will liked her.

Throughout the class she'd enjoyed watching how her nearness distracted him. It reminded her of that stunned look he'd had when she'd joked about putting out. She'd never been fond of the word *easy* for many reasons. To her, it sounded weak.

And in relationship to dating, it had become

her goal in life to make sure no man *ever* found her easy. Quite the opposite, in fact. But Will had caught her off guard. He'd surprised her because he was the last person she would have considered dating.

But he'd already ducked under her radar without bearing most of the brunt of her personality. She'd had to start giving him a hard time just so he'd know where she was coming from.

But, she also couldn't deny the fact that he had a strange effect on her. He melted her. She'd heard her sisters refer to such a feeling, but she didn't think she was capable of it. It was *she* who melted men.

If she weren't absolutely confident that she had that very same effect on Will, she might have resented these new feelings more. In fact, initially, she had. But now she had him right where she wanted him.

It was time for her to have a bit of fun.

As the last student filed out of the classroom, Melody remained leaning against the wall. Will turned to her.

"Staying late, Melody? You seemed to master the waltz just fine today. I didn't think you needed any extra help."

His words were innocent, but Melody could read the look on his face. He was happy she'd stayed.

"I'm taking my sister's wedding very seriously. I don't want her to be disappointed. And Lord knows those stuffy rich types love lame dances like the waltz—so lay it on me, brother," she said holding out her arms for him to join her frame.

"Well, I'm sure you'll be able to just bribe the band into playing some punk music to get things going."

"My mother would have a conniption—hmm, maybe that's not such a bad idea."

Will put a slow waltz on the stereo, then he walked into her arms and squared up their frame. "Now how are you ever going to get your mother to take you seriously if you keep provoking her?"

"I have to provoke her. Her world is so superficial. She judges everything by appearance…designer labels, money, status—none of those things have any real value."

Melody paused to giggle as Will missed a step and faltered for a second. "Ha, maybe I should be giving you lessons," she teased.

"Anyway, I've seen her world, and I've seen the real world. There's no place for me among all those phonies that just want to flash their bling. My friends may look like rejects from the gutter, but they have more class than any of those my mother considers the crème de la crème."

Will pulled out of her arms as the song ended.

"Your parents will definitely be proud of one thing—you've finally got a grasp of the art of ballroom dancing. Next week is our last class, and we'll review all the forms I've taught so far. Then you'll be in perfect shape for your sister's wedding."

Melody stood in the middle of the floor stunned as Will turned off the music and began packing up. She knew when she'd been dismissed.

Later that night, Will let himself into his apartment. What had he been thinking? For a few minutes, he'd actually been entertaining the idea of bringing Melody home with him.

Ever since their date, he'd been thinking about her nonstop. She'd seen to that by placing an image in his mind that he'd been artfully avoiding until that night.

He'd allowed her to torment him today. He'd arrived resigned to the fact that there was something between them. He had a policy about not interacting with students on a personal level, but rules were the last thing on a man's mind when it came to Melody.

He'd thought it would be all right to get involved because their lessons were almost over, but now he realized that would have been a mistake. They were just too different.

Different hadn't bothered him so much at first, but after today he knew that Melody would never accept his lifestyle. All the things she was running away from were all the things he was trying to achieve.

He'd been on the other side of the tracks, literally and figuratively, and he had no intentions of going back. They probably would have had little in common other than sex anyway.

Will glanced down at the phone number sitting in the wicker bowl on his coffee table. Valencia. He needed a distraction. Maybe it was time he gave her a call.

If he wanted to be the biggest fish in the ocean, he had to stop swimming in the pond.

Chapter 6

As Melody entered Isis, she tugged at the itchy pantyhose her sister had insisted she wear. She couldn't care less that the Egyptian-themed restaurant was the trendiest new spot in town. What Mel could appreciate was that Stephanie's pseudo-celebrity status had gotten them on the VIP list, precluding them from waiting in the excruciatingly long line out front.

So, trying to be on her best behavior, Mel teetered through the restaurant in her strappy gold bridesmaid shoes, wearing a black tank dress her sister had lent her. This, once again, was one of the many events that Mel had unwittingly agreed to in advance—a bridesmaids' appreciation dinner.

Knowing that Stephanie must have planned this dinner months in advance brought on a flood of guilt. There was still the matter of the bridal shower that Mel had yet to plan. At least three times a day her mother called her voice mail with shower-planning to-do items. The thought of wading through those messages, let alone carrying out the orders, made Melody physically ill. So, once again, she pushed the entire fiasco to the back of her mind. She'd work something out. Arranging cake and punch wasn't that big a deal, right?

Finally, seated at a high-backed, round, black velvet booth, Melody slipped off her shoes and sighed with relief. The other four women were busy cooing and oohing over the elegant Egyptian decor.

The restaurant was dark, with gold-trimmed black furnishings. Egyptian elements were tastefully worked in without an overdone themed feel of Disneyland or Las Vegas. Chunks of stone hung on the walls featuring large hieroglyphs, and a large mural of Isis, the goddess of fertility and motherhood, hung over the bar.

When the waiter arrived at the table, Melody took the initiative. "Okay, I think we need to start this girls' night out with a toast. Bring us a round of those High Priestess martinis." And when she spotted the eager grin on her youngest sister's face, she added hastily, "And a virgin daiquiri for Vicky."

When the drinks came, the women toasted Stephanie's upcoming wedding, and, as the drinks flowed, the toasts became sillier.

Mel raised her glass toward the mural of Isis across the room. "May Isis, the great mother of fertility, bless you and Keenan with ten children."

Stephanie nearly spat out her drink and immediately changed the subject by toasting to their handsome waiter's derriere and the free drinks he kept bringing them.

Stephanie elbowed Melody in the ribs. "I think he's got his eye on you. You should flirt with him."

"There's no *need* to flirt with him," Mel said, narrowing her eyes at her sister. "He already brought us the drinks. Besides, I don't flirt."

"He's cute and he's just your type. He could be your date for the wedding."

Stephanie was right. He *was* the type of guy

she normally dated. His dark hair was very short and spiky and he had a silver piercing in his right eyebrow. But as she watched him from across the room, she had to admit her taste in men had taken a turn lately. Smooth sophistication was the new reckless rebellion this spring.

"Sorry, he's just not doing it for me. And don't you worry about my date for the wedding, I've already got someone in mind."

Stephanie's eyes lit up. "You do? Who is it?"

Suddenly Mel realized that she'd said too much. "Vin Diesel."

"Oh," Stephanie groaned, waving her off.

Vicky sipped her frozen daiquiri and glanced over her shoulder at the handsome waiter. "Okay, if you don't want him, I'll take him."

"He's all yours, Vicky, but you can't come stay with me when mother throws you out of the house." Melody laughed and excused herself from the table. After two rounds of martinis it was time to find the ladies' room.

"A lot of people think Mariah's a diva, but when we hang out, she's just one of the girls." Valencia's glossy pink lips were almost hypnotic in their ceaseless movement.

Will smiled politely at his date, more certain with each passing minute that this evening had been a mistake. Valencia, while very attractive, had not stopped talking about herself since they'd arrived.

Will had initially been impressed that his date had whisked them to the top of the waiting list for New York's hottest new restaurant. Isis had staged its celebrity-studded grand opening only one week before and was now accepting reservations well into the next year. But, after three courses of name-dropping and preening, he was rapidly developing a headache.

"So, have you given any thought to my offer to design your space? I'd be willing to come up tonight and give you a free consultation." The sensual proposition in her tone was anything but subtle.

"Tonight isn't good for me," Will said, massaging his temples. "I actually feel a migraine coming on."

Valencia didn't bat a lash. "Oh, Donatella suffers from horrible migraines. She's been seeing this fabulous acupuncturist in the Village. I've considered seeing him myself but I'm terrified of needles."

Will's eyes darted around the restaurant for the

waiter so he could request the check. Whatever misguided impulse had led him to initiate this date was long dead. He'd thought Valencia was just the kind of woman he needed on his arm. Polish, ambition, success—he'd thought they had those things in common. But he didn't share her shallow ego-worship and naked materialism.

Sure he'd come to appreciate the finer things in life and image was important to him, but he realized that he also valued something deeper. Take Melody, for instance. She was raw and real, take her or leave her. She said exactly what she was thinking, and she didn't hide behind a pound of lip gloss and designer labels.

Thinking back to class three nights ago, he bitterly regretted the way he'd run away when she'd made her feelings known. Even though she didn't have much interest in the lifestyle he was trying to create for himself, there obviously was something to that saying, "opposites attract."

Melody and Valencia were polar opposites, and it was Melody he found attractive. Thank goodness he had one more class to let her know.

In the bathroom, Melody washed her hands and gave herself a once-over in the mirror.

"I just love your hair!"

Melody glanced over and saw a petite woman with short hair liberally applying a layer of gloss to her lips. The woman was studying her in the mirror.

Mel was used to getting compliments on her extra-long tresses. Tonight she'd smoothed back her waves and secured her ponytail with a gold rope that she'd woven around the length of the hair to her waist. "Thank you," she said politely.

"Who does you?"

"Excuse me?" Mel had never been fond of bathroom chat.

"Who's your stylist? I just have to know. My stylist Omar is fabulous. He's done Beyoncé and Ashanti, but I'm always on the lookout for someone new."

Mel resisted the urge to roll her eyes. "I don't have a stylist. I do my own hair." She despised overpriced haircuts.

"Oh, of course. Well, it looks nice anyway."

Melody followed the woman out of the bathroom trying not to give in to the temptation to stick out her foot and trip the little minx.

When the woman arrived at her table, Mel looked over to see what kind of loser had fallen for such conspicuous wiles. The moment she locked eyes with Will, Mel almost lost her balance in her uncomfortable shoes. They exchanged stunned looks, and as Will lifted his hand to wave, Melody forced her legs to move. She zipped back to her table, not daring to look back.

Melody stared at the elegant script on the door leading to Moonlight Dance Studio. Reaching out for the handle she suddenly snatched her hand back. There was no way she could go in there.

She headed back down the hallway. She'd changed her mind about attending the final class at least a dozen times. Even now that she had gotten all the way down here, she just couldn't see herself going inside…. Not after practically throwing herself at Will last week and then seeing him out with his date.

She felt like a complete fool. The last thing she needed was to look him in the eye after that.

Snorting, Melody turned on her heel and headed back for the door. There was no way she could let him think she was some kind of coward. If she didn't show up for the last class, he'd think she was jealous or something. She had to stare him dead in the eye and let him know she wasn't fazed by his having a girlfriend.

Mel conjured up the image of the tiny woman with shiny pink lips and nearly snarled with distaste. "I'd love to take her Louis Vuitton handbag and—"

"Aren't you coming in? You're late," Will called to her from the doorway.

Sucking in her breath and trying to pretend she wasn't talking to herself, Melody brushed past him without looking up.

How dare he talk to her as if nothing was wrong? How dare he stand there looking so gorgeous in his pleated slacks and his tight black T-shirt? He should at least have the decency to look guilty for sending her mixed signals.

Melody took her place across the room with the other women, but she barely listened as Will gave the class instruction. She could see her image in the mirror, and her body language was conveying all the emotions she wasn't verbalizing.

If anger were mounting an ad campaign, Mel could be the poster child. Her left hip jutted out in her black denim cutoffs, and her arms were folded across her chest. The long braids on either side of her face did nothing to soften the stern set of her lips.

All the while, her dark-rimmed eyes shot daggers at Will. Last week, Will had looked at her as if her clothes were made of cotton candy and he wanted to remove them with his tongue. Mel was aware that she wasn't the friendliest with men, but one thing she knew for sure was when one of them wanted her—and Will Coleman had wanted her.

But, after class last week, something had definitely changed. He'd probably gotten a dose of conscience for lusting after her so openly when he was clearly involved with someone else.

Will must have finished his opening demonstration because couples were shifting around the room, and he held his hand out to her. Without budging, she narrowed her eyes at him. "Mr. Coleman, I think I'll do better on my own today."

He nodded and turned on the music for the class. Melody stood stubbornly in place, not even attempting to dance.

Will crossed the room. "Miss Rush," he said, clearly mocking her with his words and sly grin, "you seem to be having difficulty with today's lesson. Should I go over it with you?"

"Not at all," she answered curtly. Then she imitated perfectly the sequence her classmates were performing. Or it would have been perfect if the heel of the army boots she'd worn out of stubbornness hadn't dragged on the floor, nearly tripping her.

"Miss Rush." Will didn't even try to hide the smug laugh that followed. "You didn't wear the right shoes today. You're going to have to dance in your socks."

"I don't want to dance in my socks." It was a childish response, she knew. But she hated to leave him with the last word.

He winked at her, clearly enjoying her discomfort, making her seethe all the more. "Suit yourself. But if you don't take off your boots, you'll have to stay after class and polish the floors."

Her eyes followed his pointing finger to the long black mark on the glossy wood floor. Silently, Mel stalked to the corner and removed her shoes, vowing that when the studio cleared that evening, Mr. Will Coleman would be receiving an earful.

This was exactly why she never chased men. They were nothing but trouble.

After removing her shoes, she watched him from the corner. It wasn't too late just to disappear and never have to see his disgustingly smug face again. What had she seen in him anyway? He certainly wasn't her type.

Maybe that's what had attracted her. Lord knew, dating her typical grungy freaks hadn't made for any long-term relationships. Not that she was in the market for a relationship. But, she *had* begun to wonder what Will was hiding under that well-groomed exterior.

She would love to ruffle him up a bit—in bed. See his clothes disheveled—scratch the clothes—the *sheets* would be disheveled. Was he a wild man in bed...or perfectly controlled and smooth the way he was on the dance floor? Curiosity had gotten the best of her last week.

But she was one cat that it wouldn't kill.

Will had been watching the emotional war raging inside Melody from the moment she'd entered the room. After they'd run into each other Saturday night, he'd been afraid she wouldn't show at all.

He'd tried to appear nonchalant when he'd poked his head into the corridor at eleven past seven, but waves of excitement and relief had washed over him when he'd found her there.

Because she'd shown up, he knew he had a chance. But she was making it painfully clear that he was going to have to work for it. He watched her warily rejoin the class after removing her shoes. She didn't want to dance with him and he didn't want to fight—fair.

He turned off the music. "Class, let me have leaders on the left, followers on the right. We're going to practice everything we've learned over the past six weeks, rotating partners."

He smiled to himself knowing that Melody not only hated rotating, but it would force her to dance with him when the time came.

"We're going to start with a fox-trot," he said, turning on the music. He crossed the room to join an older woman in the corner, knowing he'd go through three partners before he got to Melody. The rest of the men fell in line.

Will stifled a grin as he saw Joey, Mel's *favorite* dance partner, line up across from her. This was going to be fun.

He danced his partner toward the center of the room, which, as the instructor, wasn't unusual, but in this case, it allowed him a better view of Melody.

"I'm not putting up with any of your tricks tonight, you got that?" Joey said, pulling her tightly into frame.

"What I've *got* are a couple of broken fingers. If you don't loosen up, I'm going to introduce you to my knee."

"Forget this," he said, dropping her hands and backing up. "There's no way I'm dancing with you." And through the chorus of the song, Melody and Joey marked the steps without touching. Instead, they traded dirty looks and mumbled insults.

"Switch," Will called and moved to his next partner. The sooner he got over to Melody, the better. A glance over his partner's shoulder revealed that Melody was now matched up with Scott. The boy was a pushover and would no doubt let Melody lead. At least there would be no threat of violence during this stretch.

At the next rotation, Will was now directly beside Melody's partner and could look right into her face. She was ignoring him, a task made easier by the fact that her new partner was George. He was older and a very skilled dancer. The two chatted politely as she gracefully fell into step with him.

"Switch," Will called again, this time with

some hope. She'd had time to cool off and might be more willing to cooperate with him.

He reached out to bring her into his arms and immediately discovered that he'd been mistaken. "Not so much resistance, Melody. Loosen up."

Glaring at him, she let her arms become wet noodles. "That's too loose," he snapped, pulling her tighter.

She reacted to his mild show of temper. "Teacher, teacher, are you this impatient with all your students? I thought you said *anyone* could learn to dance. Here we are at the last class, and I'm afraid you may have failed miserably."

Will refused to take the bait. "Oh, Miss Rush, a man needs a willing partner to do his best work."

The snap of her gaze told him his double entendre wasn't lost on her. But he didn't wait long for her retort. "I guess it just takes a *real* man to make *me* willing."

A snicker from beside him brought Will back to his senses. A crowded classroom wasn't the right place to finish this. "Switch!"

As Will wrapped up the class, he couldn't help feeling as though he'd let Melody get the best of him. If the rest of the class hadn't been aware of the storm brewing between Melody and himself before, they certainly were now. In addition to the furtive glances they'd noticed during the remainder of class, a few of the men had dared to offer advice as they said their final goodbyes.

After thanking Will for the lessons, George had wrapped a fatherly arm around his shoulder as they walked to the door. "My Gretchen was a real spitfire when we first met. It took a lot of courting to get her attention, but it was well worth it." George pointed to Melody. "Don't let that one get away."

"Thanks, George," he said, clapping the man on the back, genuinely pleased for the support.

But when Joey made his way toward him it was a different story. "Hey, thanks, man." Joey took Will's hand in a firm grip then leaned into his ear. "You two…get a room. I've seen that type before. All they need is one good—" he performed a violent pelvic thrust "—and they fall right in line."

Thankfully, Will noted Melody engrossed in conversation with Scott and his fiancée, so she had missed that last exchange. He watched her try to slip through the door as the couple paused to say goodbye.

Will smiled politely and then excused himself

to reach around them and grab Melody's arm. The young couple took the hint and dashed out of the room waving with knowing grins.

Still holding her arm, Will closed the studio door. "Aren't we past playing these games, Melody?"

Clearly she wasn't. "I don't know what you're talking about, teacher. I don't need any extra lessons today."

Releasing her, he folded his arms across his chest. "Really? After that dismal display you gave in class, I'd have to disagree. In fact, you've proven that we might have to go all the way back to square one."

"No. I'm sorry, teacher. There will be *no* going back." And her meaning was clear.

"Well, then maybe you just need to learn something new to revive your interest." He walked over to the stereo and inserted a new CD.

Melody stood defiantly, her voice growing angrier. "Trust me, it took me five weeks to figure out that you haven't taught me *anything* that I didn't already know."

Will weathered that blow, knowing that it was coming. She was jealous of Valencia. In her mind, he'd led her on. He wanted nothing more than to disabuse her of that notion, but he had to knock the chip off her shoulder first.

Until he did that, anything he said would go in one ear and out the other. He turned on the stereo and a slow sultry tango filled the room.

Will moved over to her. "The tango. You've got to try new things. You never know when you'll find something you really like."

"The tango," Melody said flatly. "I saw it performed on TV once. The woman was smacking the crap out of the man."

"That isn't the one I'm going to teach you." He pulled her into his arms and began whispering instructions.

"It figures. Coward." Despite her harsh words, Melody allowed him to instruct her. That was all the opening he needed.

"Ah, so you like it rough, then?" He let his hands linger at her waist.

"Huh? Oh, you'll never find out."

"You're right, I won't. I definitely like it soft, and hot…and sweet. Not rough at all."

He watched her throat bob as she swallowed hard. No quick retort to that one. "Okay, now slide your knee in between mine and lean back with your arm over your head."

"Very nice," he said as she followed his instruction. With her back arched and her breasts taking center stage, Will traced a line from her waist, up her side, to the gentle mound on the side of her breast.

Melody jerked away. "What the hell are you doing? Are you seriously going to tell me that's part of the dance?"

He straightened. "In some versions."

"Wow, you have got some major mojo working because I don't even need to learn the tango for my sister's wedding." She shook her head as if to clear it. "So, just how many students get the extra-special private dance lessons? Is that how you met your girlfriend?"

"Okay, now we're getting to it. If you're referring to the woman I was out with Saturday, she's not my girlfriend."

"Oh, please don't try to tell me she's your sister, or your cousin or even a business associate."

"No, she was my date," he said, tempted to tell Melody that she was sexy when she was angry. Especially with her black bra straps drooping around her arms under two layers of tank tops.

"Aha!"

"And it didn't work out. She wasn't my type."

"No? She sure looked like your type. She looked rich and shallow and boring."

He shrugged. "Exactly. That's not my type."

"And your type is?"

He walked toward her. "Tall. Slender. Very, very *long* hair." He was close enough now to wrap one of her braids around his fist. He gently tugged her toward him. "And really, incredibly...*undeniably*..."

Melody's eyes were wide as she waited with bated breath, lips slightly parted, for his next word.

"Mean."

She gasped in outrage. "I am not mean."

He laughed, eliminating any remaining space between them. "I had to make sure you knew I was referring to you."

With that, Will did what his body had been aching to do since their very first class. He covered her full, soft lips with his own.

Chapter 7

All of the pent-up anger that Mel had been feeling flowed from her body as she returned the kiss. Will's lips were surprisingly soft as they moved over hers. Wrapping her arms around his neck, she pushed her tongue into his mouth, not ready to be completely submissive in the embrace.

His hands slid from her waist, cupping her hips to pull her closer, and she could feel him harden. Mel smiled inside. Now she would get the upper hand back.

The kiss seemed endless as she explored aggressively with her tongue while caressing his neck and the soft spot behind his ear with her fingers.

Will pulled his head away as if coming up for air. His expression was both eager and satisfied. "You're aggressive, aren't you?"

Mel gripped his neck hard. "Now you know, I do like it rough."

He leaned forward, taking her face between both hands. "But I told you I like it gentle."

He kissed her softly, nibbling at first and then deepening the kiss with sweet long sips. He gently stroked her cheek with his thumb.

Melody suddenly felt overwhelmed by his tenderness. She'd never known a man's lips could be so soft, that a kiss could be so loving and sweet. With most men, once she let them in, it was a race to the finish line. Lips, teeth, hands, nails. Raw. Passionate. The way she'd always wanted it.

But this was new. And it was…nice. Still cupping her face with one hand, Will moved his other hand from her cheek down her neck in a light stroke. His lips softly followed.

She'd never been much for that girly foreplay. It was a waste of time. But now, every place Will's lips or tongue grazed, from her chin to her shoulder, tingled with pleasure. Every stroke sent echoing vibrations to her center.

She grabbed his shoulders and leaned into him as her knees weakened. Now his hands were back at her waist tugging her double layer of tank tops out of her shorts. His hands drove under the material, circling on the bare skin of her back.

Looking over his shoulder, Mel could see their intertwined bodies in the mirror behind them. There were mirrors on every wall. A wicked thought entered her head. What would it be like to make love to him in this room surrounded by mirrors?

"Are there any more classes in here tonight?" she asked him.

He lifted his head. "No. My class is the last one in this room on Monday nights."

"Good," she said meeting his eyes. Her unspoken message was clear.

Will gently picked her up, allowing her to encircle his waist with her legs. Without saying a word, he began to move backward until he could sit on the bench against the wall behind him.

Cradling her in his lap, he kissed her again. His fingers pushed up the material of her layered tops until he'd revealed her lacy black bra. "Mmm, now this is a surprise."

Mel straightened. "Why? Didn't you ever take biology? Girls are different from boys because—"

"No, *this*," he said, plucking the clasp of her bra. "It's…very…girly." He smiled in fascination.

"What were you expecting? Camouflage?"

He finally raised his eyes back to her face. "Yeah, maybe."

She framed his face with both her hands. "Don't be disappointed. I have one of those, too." Then she leaned in to kiss him, intent on setting his mind back to the business at hand.

While she weakened him with openmouthed kisses, he freed her breasts from the delicate bra. Just as she was leaning back for him to pull her tops over her shoulders, they were startled by the sound of the door.

"Is anybody still—oops, I'm sorry!" And the door closed abruptly.

"Who was that?" Melody had buried her face in the crook of Will's neck.

"I'm sorry," Will said, hugging her close. "That was the night janitor. I forgot he might be here."

Melody straightened, untangling herself from

Will to fix her clothes. So much for her mirror fantasy.

Will continued sitting on the bench, watching her. "Are you still…? My apartment isn't, um… If you want, we can still…"

Laughing, Mel decided to put him out of his misery. "How far is your apartment?"

He stood, smiling. "A fifteen-minute cab ride."

"Let's go."

Mel had hoped to compose herself on the way over to Will's apartment, but she never got the chance. With Will's leg pressed against hers for twelve blocks, and his hand doing tantalizing things to the back of her neck, she was never able to clear her head of the fog clouding her senses.

Without ever letting her go, Will paid the cab driver, punched in his security code and directed her toward the elevator. "I've always wondered if they had security cameras hidden on these things," he said, leaning over to press a hot kiss on her lips as the doors closed them in.

"Well, if they do, we should give them a show." Melody wrapped her arms around his neck and hooked one leg around his hip. Then, what had started out as a joke became all too real as he caught her leg and pulled her in. She now had full access to his arousal, and the feel of it stole her breath.

The elevator dinged, signaling that they'd reached their floor. Mel almost stumbled trying to right herself before the doors opened. Suave and smooth as ever, Will gently settled her on her feet and then steered her out of the doors with a warm hand on her back.

Mel furiously sucked in air, unaccustomed to this feeling of being out of control. *Get it together,* she ordered herself as Will let her into his apartment.

The room was cavernous and suited him well. It was furnished with sofas and chairs with square cushions and boxy wooden frames and dark rectangular tables, smooth, clean and modern in hues of cream, tan and coffee-brown.

Her perusal was cut short as Will pulled her back into his arms. "Would you like something to drink?"

She looked into his eyes and shook her head.

"Hungry?"

"Nope."

"Good." His lips covered hers and heat immediately began rising within her. She felt like a hot, steamy mess and Will still seemed cool and in control.

And that bothered her.

Wanting to see him mussed and reckless, she growled and began pulling and tugging at the shirt neatly tucked in his waistband.

He caught her rapidly moving hands in his own. "Still want to play rough, huh? Okay, maybe just this once."

Before Mel could figure out what was happening, Will had scooped her up into his arms and was carrying her—thanks to Mel's height, something that rarely had been attempted and was always regretted.

Then she was falling. She bounced lightly as her back hit the soft mattress underneath her. Will came down on top of her and she was forced to stop thinking.

The heady scent of his masculine cologne filled her nostrils. Her boots were already gone. He raked her shorts and tights down her legs and she kicked her feet free of them. Her hands slid inside his shirt to find the soft smooth skin of Will's bare chest.

With a desperate groan, he unfastened his pants and shoved them down just far enough to free himself. Then he was inside her, and she couldn't have been more ready for him.

Will woke thirty minutes before his alarm the next morning. Reaching out, careful not to wake Melody, he flicked the tab that turned off the buzzer.

He shook his head as his chest instantly filled with regret. They'd barely even gotten their clothes off last night. He'd wanted so badly to make love to Melody properly. Romantically.

She didn't seem to require romance, but Will's heart told him that she needed it.

Instead he'd given in to some primitive instinct for immediate gratification. He'd hoped to fit in a second time, but they'd barely gotten the rest of their clothes off before they'd fallen asleep. She'd made him lose control. But, to his surprise, he'd really liked it.

Over the past several weeks, he'd fallen into a dry routine, but being with Melody had made him feel alive again. She reminded him of what it had been like just to hang out and be himself with his family and his boys from the old neighborhood.

In this new world he was living in, he had to

live in the right neighborhood, drive the right car and know the right people. He'd gone to great pains to fit in. He was always on point, saying and doing all the right things.

But last night, he'd been able to let go, able to release himself and just be free. It was a feeling he'd tried to hold on to in his life by continuing to dance, but he'd reached a new understanding of freedom in Melody's arms.

Still, he had regrets. He hadn't wanted last night to be all about him. He'd planned to take his time, show her tenderness, maximize her pleasure by making sure she was completely ready.

At least, she hadn't complained. On the contrary, she'd very noisily assured him of her satisfaction. He'd never gone in for wild bedroom hijinks, but Will had to admit, it had done wonders for his ego to know he could make Melody scream. She'd held nothing back.

Will stared at the clock. He had to get ready to go to work, but he didn't want to leave her. Part of him was afraid that once she left his sight, he'd never see her again. They no longer had dance classes together, and Melody was so unpredictable. For all he knew, this was a one-night stand for her.

* * *

Melody came awake with a start. Someone was shaking her shoulders. "Huh, what? I'm awake."

Blinking rapidly, she finally brought Will's face into focus. And then the rest of him. He was fully dressed in shirt and tie with his coat folded over his arm.

She sat up. The sheet covering her slid down, leaving her naked to the waist, but she barely noticed. "What's up?"

"Melody, I have to go to work now, but I want you to stay. Will you be here when I get back?"

Sucking in a deep breath, Mel tried to pump oxygen to her brain. She looked around, trying to get her bearings. She instantly remembered that she and Will had slept together last night. She smiled.

"Um, will I be here?" She scratched her head. She was not a morning person. Her brain didn't usually kick in until after nine and the giant numbers on Will's digital clock read 6:47.

Will was sitting on the edge of the bed and he leaned toward her, speaking more slowly. "There's fresh coffee in the kitchen if you'd like some, but you don't have to get up now. I just wanted to let you know that I'm leaving, and find out if you had plans—anywhere you had to be today—because I was hoping you'd stay. I'd really like to see you when I get home tonight."

Melody tried to think, but her mind was blissfully blank. Issue number sixty-three of Delilah was on schedule, so she was probably free. "Yeah, I guess I don't have anywhere to be."

Even through her bleary eyes and sleep-hazed state, Mel could not miss the effect her statement had on Will. His face broke into a huge smile of happiness and…relief?

"Huuh-hmmm," she yawned. "Did I see a big-screen TV in your living room?"

"Yes, and I have satellite TV with more than five hundred channels."

"Yeah, I'll be here," she said, letting her head fall back onto the pillows. Will kissed her goodbye, telling her he'd be back by five, but she barely heard him as she drifted back to sleep.

Chapter 8

Mel couldn't bear to drag herself out of bed until half past noon. There was something about Will's bed that made her want to linger there. She'd heard Stephanie rave about Egyptian-cotton sheets and down pillows, but Melody hadn't put much stock in such things—until now.

Will's bed must have been outfitted with only the best, because right now, as she spread herself out on the soft sheets, she felt like she was being cradled in a cloud.

Suddenly Melody sat straight up in bed. Whoa.

She had to get a grip on herself. She'd run into trouble once already when she let herself go all mushy for this guy. A trip to the shower was what she needed. That would clear her head.

But instead, as hot water streamed over her from dual shower heads, Mel slipped further into the lap of luxury. Somewhere in the back of her head she knew she could have provided many of these comforts for herself, but she'd always taken a certain pride in not relying on minor conveniences.

Mel had never fit the mold of a trust-fund baby, anyway. She had a decent relationship with her father, but her mother controlled the purse strings. And that relationship was tumultuous enough that she secretly expected to be disinherited by thirty. Besides, she was an artist—and artists were destined to suffer.

For today, drinking burnt coffee from Will's fancy coffeemaker would be the extent of her suffering. She'd briefly considered making a fresh pot, but there were so many knobs and buttons, she didn't have the patience to figure it out.

As the warmth and caffeine of the coffee began to fire up her neurons, Melody could no longer ignore the rumbling in her stomach. "What's he got in here to eat?" she wondered out loud, moving toward the refrigerator.

The narrow kitchen was outfitted with matching black-and-white appliances, some of which she recognized—coffeemaker, toaster oven—and some of which she didn't.

"What is that? Some kind of food processor?" she asked no one in particular, staring at a large black box with a clear plastic container mounted on top.

Melody was no whiz in the kitchen on her best day, but it was an understatement to say Will's set-up was more sophisticated than most. More out of curiosity than a genuine desire to cook, Mel studied Will's stove with rapt fascination.

Close inspection revealed that there were no protruding knobs or buttons *anywhere* on the stove—just a large LCD panel that displayed the time and date.

"Wow, there's no way to turn this thing on," she muttered, running her hands over the smooth brushed steel.

Suddenly the time and date cleared from the digital panel and were replaced with a greeting message.

"Good afternoon!" said a female voice from the stove.

Melody leapt back so far she banged into the counter, knocking over a spice rack. Holding a hand to her heaving chest, Mel surveyed the demon stove before her. "Good Lord, how do I turn this freaking thing off?" she shouted.

Immediately, the digital display blinked off, and Melody ran out of the kitchen, vowing never to go back.

Later, still wrapped in nothing but Will's warm terrycloth robe, Mel ate grapes by the handful in front of the wide-screen TV. Her angry stomach had overcome her fear of the stove, and she'd raided the refrigerator for non-cook items.

By two o'clock, Melody had begun to get bored. It was amazing how, even with five hundred channels, she couldn't find anything on television to hold her interest. Rising from the sofa, Mel began to prowl around the apartment.

Melody wandered into the spare bedroom Will used as an office. Sitting down with a sheet of typing paper, she found herself sketching Will.

This time, instead of focusing on his face, she concentrated on his body. Melody now had intimate knowledge of every smooth ridge of muscle cording his body. As her fingers transferred their tactile memories to paper, she automatically sheathed him in the form-fitting unitard of a comic-book hero. Will was the closest thing to a superhero she'd ever encountered in real life.

He moved with the fluidity and grace of a cat. And, he had lightning-quick reflexes, which she had discovered on the dance floor every time she'd stumbled and he'd caught her.

The sudden trill of the telephone ringing interrupted her thoughts.

Her first instinct was to ignore it. But what if Will needed to reach her? A slow smile spread across her face at the thought of another possibility. The hope that it could be Will's date from the restaurant made her snatch up the phone with wicked anticipation.

"Hello?"

"Melody, I'm glad you picked up," Will said from the other end of the line.

"Oh, it's you."

He snorted. "Thanks, I missed you, too."

"Sorry. By the way, did you know your stove is possessed?"

He laughed. "Oh yeah, I should have warned you about that. These apartments are outfitted with ultramodern appliances."

"No kidding. I nearly had a heart attack when the stove started talking to me."

"One of these days I need to read the manual on that thing. Needless to say, I eat out a lot."

"Smart man."

"Listen, I'm calling because something's come up here at the office. One of the associates just made partner and we're all expected to attend a cocktail party in his honor."

"No problem, I'll just head back downtown."

"Actually, I was hoping you'd come down to the restaurant and meet me."

Mel's mind went blank. "What do you mean? After everyone leaves?"

"No, it's being held at the bar on the ground floor of my office building. I just need to make an appearance there. Then we can leave and do whatever you want."

She stared at the phone as though it were a foreign object. "Will, you know the only clothes I have with me are the ones I came over wearing."

He paused for a second. "I know. If you want, my washer and dryer is located behind the door off from the kitchen. And feel free to steal anything you want from my closet. You're an artist, I know you can pull something together with your typical flare. I don't care what you have on, I just want to see you."

Melody got directions and hung up the phone. A mix of emotions flooded her mind. The first and strongest feeling was flattery.

He trusted her to show up in whatever crazy getup she could pull together. Will really *got* her. Nothing in his tone implied that he expected her to run down to Saks and buy something more suitable. He was letting her know he accepted her just the way she was.

And while the largest part of her was flattered that Will wanted to see her no matter how she showed up looking, another part of her—the rebellious part—was challenged. Didn't he think she *could* clean up well? Her previous failed attempt aside, just because she chose to buck the trends didn't mean she wasn't able to make herself presentable when necessary.

A wicked grin formed on her lips. It was perfect that he was expecting her to show up with her "typical flair" as he'd put it. But Will was in for a surprise.

Will stationed himself near the opening to the private room in the Minute Man Pub where Paul

Bellemy, the investment firm's newest partner, hosted a happy hour in his own honor. The public area of the bar was teeming with people, but for the most part he could see the door.

"You keep watching the door like a hawk, Coleman. Who the hell are you waiting for?" his colleague Mark Branson asked, peering over his shoulder.

"I have a date coming. I just want to make sure she can find us back here."

"A date?" Mark slapped Will hard on the back. "Buddy, when are you going to learn? Bringing a date to the Minute Man is like bringing pizza to a barbecue. Aren't the girls around here hot enough for you?"

Will resisted the urge to roll his eyes at Mark. The guy was always on the prowl, but as far as Will could tell, he never actually got any action. "Branson, when you have filet mignon at home, why bother eating at a barbecue?"

"Well, if she's really that hot, maybe I'll stand here and wait with you. I'll check out the goods for you. Give you my stamp of approval."

Will turned away from the door, trying to direct Mark's attention back to the throng surrounding Paul Bellemy. "You might want to get over there and grab some face time with Bellemy. Find out how he wrangled his way into Robert Geddes's golf circle."

Just then, another colleague, Chris Walters, walked up. "I already beat that horse to death. Bellemy's not giving up any info."

"Besides," Mark chimed in, still looking over Will's shoulder, "I think I see something I like."

Will turned and the first things he noticed were a sexy pair of shoes. They were black sandals that crisscrossed up shapely legs, stopping just below a pair of sculpted calves. From there his gaze climbed the long dark legs to the jagged gossamer hem of a black cocktail dress. When his sights zeroed in on the woman's narrow waist and the cascade of silky dark hair that surrounded it, he knew he was looking at Melody.

Like a rocket, his gaze shot to her face. Then he simply gaped like a fool as she continued toward him. Her halter dress revealed a deep V of cleavage. Not enough to be scandalous, but just enough to tease him with a hint of the supple brown mounds beneath the gauzy fabric. The hair at her temples had been pulled away from her face with gold clips, allowing the rest to stream down her back in glossy waves. As usual,

Melody's eyes were darkly lined, but now they were highlighted with a smokey shadow. And he couldn't help but notice those shiny bronzed lips.

From somewhere in the back of his imagination, Will heard an announcer's voice-over. *Will doesn't know it yet, but we've secretly replaced his regular Melody with this supermodel version. Let's see if he notices.*

"Melody?" Will croaked incredulously.

"The one and only," she said, sauntering over. When she reached the doorway where they stood, her heel faltered and she slid into Will's side.

All three men reached out to steady her. She gently batted the other men away. "Don't mind me, first day on the new feet. But, Will's used to my clumsiness. Can you believe that for the last five weeks this man has been teaching me to dance?"

"I didn't know that," Chris answered.

"Lucky bastard," Mark said. "Since when do you dance?"

Melody raised a hand to her lips. "Oops, was that a secret?"

Feeling himself flush, Will tried to explain himself. "It's not a secret, it just never came up in office conversation," he said to Melody, then turned to his colleagues. "I teach ballroom dancing twice a week. It's a hobby."

Mark's eyes were still locked on Melody. "And that's how you met this beautiful woman? Where do I sign up?"

Will swallowed hard. He'd never been the jealous type, but the way Mark was eyeing Melody made him want to dump his drink over the guy's head.

He didn't know why he'd never mentioned his dancing to his coworkers. Yes, things were hectic at the office, but there had been plenty of occasions like this one for him to have mentioned it. But, for some reason, he hadn't felt that any of them would have been able to relate to the fact that he needed something that brought peace, something he had control over.

When it was time to discuss trendy night spots, car accessories or expensive vacations, Will lined up to share. Office chatter was all just an adult version of show-and-tell anyway. But his dancing? He hadn't wanted to taint that part of his life with any snide remarks or crude jokes about getting to grope women.

Will wrapped his arm around Melody's waist and began to move away. "I hope you gentleman will excuse us while I escort the lady to the bar for a drink."

The men made noises of protest, but Will didn't break his stride.

"Can't get away from those jerks fast enough, huh?" Melody whispered in his ear.

"Something like that," he answered with a soft laugh. He paused halfway to the bar to fully admire her. "Where did you get these clothes? You look amazing, but it's not what I was expecting at all."

Melody's grin was smug. "Saks Fifth Avenue—it's great for one-stop shopping. When I first walked in wearing my cutoffs, I thought they were going to pull a *Pretty Woman* on me. But, those chicks weren't fazed. I figure with the influx of wealthy rappers and rock stars, they've seen everything by now."

Will couldn't take his eyes off her. "You didn't have to go to all of that trouble for me. It's just a happy hour. I wanted you to feel comfortable."

"Don't worry about me, I know the drill. My father's a politician, remember? These are your business associates, therefore, their first impression of me reflects upon you. I guess some of my mother's teachings are more deeply ingrained than I thought," she said sheepishly.

Will felt a rush of pride at Melody's words. It meant a lot to him that she was concerned enough about his career that she would go to all this trouble. "What can I get you to drink?"

He saw her gaze upward, as though mentally running the list. "Honestly, I'd love a beer."

He got her a beer and the same for himself. After taking a sip, he finally began to relax.

"Okay, so fill me in on what's going on here," Melody asked.

"In a nutshell, Bellemy was just promoted to partner and we're celebrating."

"Cool. When will you be in line to become a partner?"

Will laughed. "Not for many years, if ever. I'd have to pay my dues at the firm, make some huge investments, reel in some big whales, uh, clients…"

"Oh, so this Bellemy guy did all that? He looks like he's fresh out of college."

"Actually, he might have skipped a few steps."

She raised her brows. "What do you mean?"

"The firm's president, Robert Geddes, has this private golf game. It's impossible to get an invitation, but, if you do, big things start happening for your career."

Melody grinned. "Golf, huh? Do you play?"

"I started taking lessons, you know, just in case. But, far bigger suck-ups than me have tried and failed to get that invitation. I'm afraid I'm going to have to make it the old-fashioned way."

After they'd finished their drinks, Will was amazed at how Melody went to work on the room. He'd expected they'd make the rounds quickly and head out, but she'd insisted on staying. Obviously, being the daughter of a politician had had an impact on her, because she mingled like a pro. Not only was she absolutely stunning, but she was charming as well. And she never missed an opportunity to talk him up.

When he couldn't stall a visit to the men's room any longer, he knew she'd be fine on her own. In fact, she'd taken on the weight of most of the conversation anyway. His colleagues were fascinated by her.

To his surprise, when he returned, Melody was on a first-name basis with Robert Geddes. Will hadn't yet had any face time with the bigwig because he'd been tightly surrounded by the company's best brownnosers. Now he gently breached the crowd to reach Melody.

"It's true, Rob," she was saying. "Ever since my father played in a charity tournament with

Tiger, my mother frequently calls upon him to participate in her inner-city youth outreach program."

Will felt his mouth go dry. Did she just call his boss Rob?

"That's fantastic. I've always wanted to meet Tiger Woods," Geddes said.

Melody glanced over her shoulder at Will. "Oh good, here's Will. Rob and I were just talking about golf. You play, don't you?" She pulled him into her space and backed away. "Excuse me, it's my turn to hit the ladies' room."

Later that evening at a pizza parlor near Will's apartment, Melody tugged her shoes off under the table. "Oh, man, I don't think I'll ever be able to wear shoes again. My feet are swollen to the size of basketballs."

"My bathtub has jets. I'll take you home and rub them for you, then you can take a nice long soak."

She raised her brows at him. "What makes you think that I'll be going home with you again tonight?"

"Did you hear what I just said? Foot massage and hot tub. Need I say more?"

"Not really, no," Mel said after a brief pause. "I just don't want you thinking I'm moving in or anything. I have to go back to my apartment tomorrow."

"Something pressing calling you back?"

Mel rolled her eyes. "I have less than a week to put a bridal shower together from scratch."

Will's brow wrinkled. "Less than a week? How did you get so far behind?"

Melody felt her cheeks heat. "For the last couple of weeks my mother's been calling me and barking orders at me for the shower."

"And…?"

"And I ignored her. It's insulting for someone to make it painfully clear that they have no faith in you. Of course, I set myself up to prove her right by organizing absolutely nothing. The only thing that's been done so far are the invitations."

"Well, that's something, right?"

"My mother sent them. So, without a doubt there will be ninety of my mother's closest friends and associates at the Ritz Carlton Sunday afternoon. But, as of right now, they'll be showing up to an empty room."

Will whistled through his teeth. "Have you at least attended a lot of bridal showers?"

"Not since I was younger, and I wasn't paying much attention at the time."

"I'll tell you one thing, no matter how the shower turns out, your mother would be proud of the way you worked that cocktail party tonight. You met more people at the firm in one evening than I've met in my five years working there. And thanks to you, I'm now on a first-name basis with the head honcho."

Arm-in-arm, with Mel carrying her shoes, they walked back to Will's apartment. Although Will made good on his promise for a foot massage, he didn't stop with her feet. And it was a good while before they got around to soaking in the hot tub.

Chapter 9

Melody had just placed the last handwritten place card on the last silver charger plate when the hotel event coordinator rushed up to her.

"A week ago I never would have believed this was possible, but I think we've pulled it off." The spunky blonde surveyed the room as if it were a miracle. "I just saw your first guests arriving in the lobby."

Melody reached out and squeezed her hand. "Thanks for all you've done, Sharon. I couldn't have put this shower together at the last minute without you."

She'd relied heavily on the other woman's professional expertise for details that Mel never would have thought of—like giving out bags of cookies shaped like designer dresses for party favors.

"Thanks to your liberal budget, making last-minute magic was a lot easier. But, I have to give you credit, it's your ideas and creativity that will really impress the bride."

The artist in Melody had kicked in at the eleventh hour, and she'd actually begun to enjoy the preparations. Using Keenan's bridesmaid dress sketches for inspiration, Mel had stayed up late into the night drawing wispy images of Stephanie and Keenan on six large white art boards. They were now set up around the room on easels as the finishing touch to Melody's fashion-show theme.

In just a few minutes, the first guests would be able to strut down the runway at the entrance to their tables on the other side of the room. At the center of each table was an arty arrangement of handbags and shoes from Stephanie's favorite designers.

Mel hoped against hope that no one would

realize they were knockoffs she'd wrangled from street vendors in Times Square.

"Oh, my gosh, everything looks amazing."

Melody whirled around, discovering, to her relief, that the bride herself was the first to arrive with bridesmaids Lana and Jessica in tow. The models dropped their presents on the gift table and immediately began working the runway, while Stephanie barreled around the head of the T-shaped runway to the seating area where Melody stood.

Within seconds Melody found herself in a crushing hug. "Mother told me not to get my hopes up, but I knew you'd come through for me. You always have. This is just perfect."

Melody caught Sharon's eye over Stephanie's shoulder. Sharon winked at her, mouthing the words, "I told you," before slipping out the door.

After that, it was a whirlwind of activity as guests began arriving. Most of the attendees, professional models and amateurs alike, enjoyed making their grand entrance down the runway to the funky hip-hop music playing over the speakers. When they reached the stairs, all the seated guests would applaud and cheer.

Although some shy relatives and older friends

of the family chose to sneak around the side, avoiding the runway altogether, overall, Melody heard nothing but raves, confirming that her fashion-show theme was a success.

As she waited at the entrance greeting guests, Melody couldn't help noticing that her mother was conspicuously absent.

Finally, forty-five minutes late, Beverly Rush appeared. She paused, taking everything in, and then deftly took the runway, stopping halfway down to peel of her white suit jacket, revealing her sleeveless crepe top. Slinging the jacket over her shoulder, she switched her hips across the narrow stage and stopped at the end in an elegant flourish.

All the guests rose, giving her a standing ovation. The mother of the bride had arrived.

Melody tried to play the good hostess by visiting every table to chat with the guests. By far, the most popular question was who would be her date for the wedding. Trying to keep it light, she offered one outrageous response after another.

"Well, Aunt Thea, my boyfriend Bill was all set to leave his wife until the press started hinting that she'd run for president. Until the media attention dies down, I'll probably have to attend the wedding alone."

Melody was busy refilling her plate at the buffet table when her sister Vicky rushed over to her. "Now that Mom's finally here, do you want to start the games?"

"Games? What are you talking about?"

Vicky shook her head in frustration. "The shower games. Oh, my God, don't tell me you didn't plan any shower games."

Melody felt her eyes go wide. "Nobody told me we had to play games. I though we just stuffed our faces and talked for a couple of hours. Then Stephanie opens her gifts, we eat some cake and go home."

Vicky began to wring her hands. "Everyone is expecting to play at least a game or two. Can't you think of something?"

Melody rolled her eyes. She couldn't remember the last time she'd had to attend a bridal shower, let alone any games they might have played.

"I'm not sure this is the right crowd for the games I know how to play." Refusing to fail now, Mel shoved her plate at Vicky. "This might not be pretty, but I'll see what I can do."

Standing at the head of the T-shaped runway, Melody clapped her hands to get the room's attention. "Okay, everyone, please take a moment to make sure you have a full glass of punch or champagne in front of you, we're getting ready to play some games."

By five o'clock that evening, the shower was over and guests were filing out of the ballroom. Melody stood at the entrance where she collected accolades for throwing the most lively shower many of them had ever attended.

She felt a little wave of guilt as a tipsy Aunt Thea, singing Snoop Dog's "Drop It Like It's Hot" under her breath, had to be escorted out between her embarrassed daughters.

Stephanie came up behind her, tugging her arm to pull her aside. "That was amazing, but can I ask you a question? Were those drinking games we were playing?"

Melody felt her face flush. "Um…"

They *had* been drinking games, and Mel had been pleasantly surprised at how well they'd gone over. She had each woman competing against the other women at her table for the shoes and handbags in the centerpieces. After three different games, all the prizes had been awarded and the guests were either happy winners or too tipsy to care.

"That's okay, don't tell me," Stephanie said. "I had a fantastic time. You gave me more than I could ever have hoped for."

Mel felt her chest swell. Suddenly she wished this event had been less happy accident and more diligent planning. Her sister deserved it. Before she could find the words to express that sentiment to her sister, their mother approached them. Mel had begun to wonder if Beverly was planning to go through the entire shower without acknowledging her.

Melody braced herself. Stephanie, obviously sensing what was coming, tried in vain to direct the conversation. "I was just telling Melody what a wonderful job she did with the shower. Don't you agree, Mother?"

Beverly turned her head and gave the room another once-over. She was smiling, so Mel got suckered into expecting a positive response.

"Yes, well, I just would have hoped that today, of all days, you would have made *some* effort to dress appropriately." She reached out to finger the mandarin collar of Melody's black jumpsuit.

Melody looked down at her clothes. The form-fitting black jumpsuit was tied off just below her knees, leaving plenty of room to show off her knee-high, shiny black boots. The top was open to the waist, revealing a fuchsia T-shirt with the word *diva* printed across the chest.

She'd even painstakingly piled her hair atop her head just to prove to her mother that it could be done. She'd anchored the elaborate curly updo with a million bobby pins and two fuchsia chopsticks. She'd thought the look was stylish and hip for a fashion-themed shower.

Melody held up the digital camera hanging around her neck. "I dressed for the theme, Mother. I'm supposed to be a fashion photographer."

Beverly shook her head. "Speaking of the theme, this is not the traditional Victorian high tea we discussed. Why, I never would have chosen the Ritz Carlton if I'd known you weren't going to do the tea. There are so many other sites better suited to…"

All Melody heard after that was "blah, blah, blah." She kept telling herself that her mother's approval was something she was never going to get and it was a waste of time even to seek it. She thought she'd learned that lesson when she was eight years old and she'd been awarded first place in the fourth-grade art show.

Her mother had patted her head and offered a tepid, "That's nice, dear, but make sure you focus on subjects that are really important. You can't make a career out of art." Melody had cried that night, but today her eyes were dry. They stayed dry all the way to Will's apartment.

As he opened the door, a wide smile spread across his face. "Ah, there you are. I thought you were going to call first, but this is much better," he said, pulling her into his arms for a long, languid kiss.

Melody immediately began to feel desire stirring below. Opening her mouth, she slipped her tongue into his. Then she began pushing him forward, out of the doorway, as she began to tug at the T-shirt tucked into his jeans.

"Whoa, Melody, slow down there. You're starting to make me think you just want me for my body," he said, reaching around her to shut the apartment door.

In the week since their first encounter, they'd spent nearly every night together. "So what if I do? Is that a problem?" she asked, continuing to tug on his T-shirt.

Will paused for a moment. "No. Not really." Then he backed up to the sofa and pulled her onto his lap.

Mel felt a wave of satisfaction as she finally got Will's T-shirt over his head. *Did* she just want him for his body? Probably not, but for the moment it was the part of him that held the most interest for her. For a stockbroker/dance instructor his body was solidly packed with muscles. She'd never been with a man with such a hard body before.

She ran her hands over the rippling expanse of chocolate-brown skin. No tattoos. She liked tattoos, but she had to admit that it would be a crime to mar the perfection that was Will's skin.

She found the dark pebbles that were his nipples and let them tickle her palms. Will just leaned back, closed his eyes and let her have complete control.

Melody unsnapped his jeans and pulled at his zipper, but she didn't feel like struggling to take his pants off. So she slid to one side, off his lap and commanded, "Take those off."

Will complied silently and when he stood before her in just his boxer briefs, Melody took a moment to enjoy the view. "Okay, now those, too."

He shimmied out of them slowly and then

swung them around his finger to add a bit of strip-tease flare. "Now, what about you?"

"What about me?" She propped her high-heeled boots on the coffee table and splayed her hands.

With a wicked arch of the brow, Will bent to remove her boots. Then he removed her jumpsuit, her T-shirt and her underwear. Taking full advantage of the situation, he rubbed, stroked, caressed and kissed everywhere he bared skin.

By the time Melody was fully nude before him, her body was humming with anticipation. She loved the feel of his rough masculine hands on the soft skin of her body. Everywhere he touched, he left her aching for more.

Finally, she straddled him. "Be still," she commanded, trying to regain the upper hand.

Bending her head, she molded her mouth over his, inserting her tongue to kiss him in a way that she knew made him crazy.

When she felt his hands grip her bottom urgently and heard that telling moan of pleasure, she knew she was back in charge. The only problem was that the feel of his naked body, smooth skin encasing steely muscle, was getting the best of her, too.

It was so hard to think when she could smell

his musky scent and hear his rapid breathing. Nothing turned her on more than knowing that she was wanted.

"Melody," Will gasped as his fingers found her sensitive core.

All control slipped away as passion spiked inside her. "Oh, Will, now. I need you now."

Will groped for the jumbo box of condoms that was still sitting on the coffee table from their trip to the drug store a few days ago.

When he was ready, Melody moved herself into position to lower herself onto him. As he filled her up, she slid her arms around his neck and clung to him.

With his strong hands guiding her bottom, she rocked, rolled and writhed, releasing all of her tensions into the moment.

Holding nothing back, she tilted her face to the ceiling and cried out her pleasure. Will began thrusting upward aggressively. Melody knew her uninhibited sounds drove him over the edge of excitement.

As she began to grow tired, Will stood, holding her against him. He laid her on her back on the couch and continued thrusting.

Gratification hit Melody suddenly like a

powerful blow. Her body slammed against the cushions, her back arched. "Will!" she yelled, feeling her body convulse with an intense pleasure.

Will was already in the throes of his own satisfaction, as he buried his face in her neck and sighed against her. Quiet and neat. Just like the man.

After a brief rest, they went in for round two, ending in the bedroom. Will rolled over, staring into the face of a now deeply relaxed Melody.

"You know, going to the gym works exactly the same way."

Melody didn't open her eyes. "What are you talking about?"

"I'm talking about stress relief. I've noticed you use sex to work out your tension. And you must have had a lot of tension, because I haven't had the strength to visit the gym in almost two weeks."

She snorted. "Maybe I'm just a very…lusty woman. Are you saying you can't keep up?"

"I'm saying I get the feeling the bridal shower didn't quite go as planned."

Her eyes snapped open. "Now that's where

you're wrong, Dr. Freud. The shower was a great success. My sister couldn't have been happier. And that's all that really matters."

"Aha," he said, nodding.

"What?" She scowled.

"That's all that really matters...what does that mean? That there was someone who *could* have been happier?"

Melody rolled over, giving Will her back.

"Was it your mother?" he pressed.

"I've told you about her. She's never satisfied with anything."

"Is that **true**? Or is she just never satisfied with anything that *you* do?"

"That one," Melody muttered.

"And that bothers you?"

She rolled onto her back. "Seriously, quit psychoanalyzing me. My mother doesn't get me. She never will, and I've accepted that."

Will opened his mouth to respond.

"And if you ask, 'Have you?' I swear to God I'll hit you."

He closed his mouth so quickly his teeth clattered. After a moment of silent contemplation between them, he decided to try again. "All mothers are difficult. It's their job. That doesn't mean they don't love you."

Melody turned to face him. "When you say all mothers are difficult, I think you mean that they complain when it rains too much, or expect you to drive for an hour just to carry groceries in from the car. You don't know my mother."

Will waited for her to continue, and just when he thought she might not go on, she began to speak.

"She's a joy, she's a dream. She's the pinnacle of class and manners. Everyone loves Beverly Rush. The woman only gets cranky when it comes to me. She heaps praise and adoration on my sisters. Me? I'm Cinderella. I think she's forgotten that I'm her firstborn—the one she's supposed to dote on."

Will felt his heart swell for Melody. Her tough exterior was beginning to make a lot more sense. All her life she'd felt that she had something to prove to her mother. When she'd finally decided that was a futile effort, she'd gone as far in the opposite direction as one could go. Then she stared you down and all-out dared you not to accept her the way she was.

"People have strange reasons for acting the

way they do," Will said, determined to say his piece and change the subject. "All I know is, your mother *does* love you—"

Her disgruntled snort interrupted him. "You only think that because in your world, there's always a happy ending, and mothers love all their children equally. But I live in the—"

Will reached out and placed a silencing finger over her rapidly-moving lips. "You didn't let me finish. I was going to say that it's impossible to resist loving you, Melody Rush. I know that, because *I'm* falling in love with you."

Will watched her face carefully. He wasn't expecting reciprocation. Quite the opposite, in fact. He expected her to make some smart remark about him being a sap.

Instead he noticed that her body had gone still. As she looked up at him, her lashes began blinking rapidly. Dear Lord, her eyes were welling with tears.

She tried valiantly to fight it by darting her eyes around and turning away, until finally she gave in. Clapping both hands over her face, she turned into the pillow and sobbed violently.

"Oh, my God, Melody. I'm sorry. Baby, what's wrong?"

Terror-stricken, Will rubbed her back as she continued to cry. Finally, when the tears subsided, she raised her head, taking the tissue he offered her.

"Are you all right?" he asked, realizing that she was mortified by her emotional reaction.

She sniffed, reaching out to punch him in the arm lightly. "Yeah, but why did you have to make me go all girly, saying things like that?"

He sighed. "Because I love you."

Melody leaned forward and burrowed her head into his chest, hugging him tightly. And Will knew she loved him, too.

Chapter 10

Melody's alarm went off at 6:00 a.m. on the day of her sister's wedding. The ceremony wouldn't start for another twelve hours, but she had a full schedule of hair, makeup, photos and other maid-of-honor duties to contend with.

Brain barely functional, Mel made a beeline for the shower, and just as she was about to turn on the life-effusing spray, the phone rang.

Cursing savagely, Melody stepped out of the tub, nearly tripping. She made a mad, naked dash for the cordless phone, certain her sister was already in some sort of wedding crisis. With any luck the wedding was canceled and she could go back to bed.

"What is it?" she barked into the receiver, closing her tired eyes.

"Finally! Geez, don't you check your messages anymore?"

Melody's eyes snapped open as she stared at the phone like a foreign object. "Bass? What the hell—it's six in the morning."

"I wouldn't have had to call so early if you'd called me back. The wedding's today, isn't it?"

"Yeah, I was just starting to get ready."

"Well, you haven't gotten back to me about any of the details. I just went ahead and borrowed the red tuxedo jacket we talked about. And I found this killer ruffled flamenco shirt at the Salvation Army."

As Bass spoke Mel felt her entire body go hot with embarrassment. How could she have forgotten that she'd invited Bass to be her date months ago—long before she'd met Will? They'd had a ball dreaming up scandalous outfits for him to wear just to freak everyone out.

Wincing, she chewed on her lower lip trying to figure out how to explain that things had changed.

The urge to make a statement on Stephanie's big day had long passed. While she'd always gotten along with her younger siblings, the wedding activities had given them an opportunity to genuinely bond.

"Oh, God, Bass. I don't know how to tell you this. There's been a change in plans."

"What is it? I've been leaving you messages for over a week. Since you didn't respond I assumed the original plan was still a go."

Melody's guilt rose up in her throat strong enough to nearly choke her. She'd been severely neglecting her friends. In fact, last night had been the first she'd spent in her own apartment in weeks. She'd stumbled in from the rehearsal dinner after midnight and had gone straight to sleep.

"Bass, the reason I've been so scarce lately is that I've been seeing someone." She held her breath waiting for his reaction.

Even though it had been nearly two years since there had been anything other than friendship between them, she'd avoided telling Bass about Will. Although he'd had a front-row seat to her other few and fleeting romances, things were very different with Will. She wasn't ready to receive judgment on this relationship.

"Well, I owe Tha twenty bucks. She said you were probably getting laid, but I said you would have told us if you were seeing a new guy."

She heard the disappointment in his voice and more guilt welled up inside her. "He's my dance instructor. I didn't want to mention anything to you guys because I knew there would be a lot of ribbing about it."

She heard a heavy sigh on the other end of the phone. "So, you're taking this *dance* instructor to the wedding?"

"Yes. I'm sorry." Mel couldn't remember a time she'd ever felt worse. She briefly considered calling Will to explain her prior arrangements, but dismissed that thought immediately. Bass wouldn't really want to spend the evening with her family. He disliked them more than they disliked him. This type of thing was much more Will's speed.

"What is he? Some clean-cut, smooth operator your family would approve of?"

"Probably, but that has nothing to do—"

"It's okay, I get it now."

His tone spoke volumes and Melody's guilt was temporarily displaced by rising anger. "What is that supposed to mean?"

"You disappear for weeks. You cut off all of your friends. Now I find out it's because you're dating your high-society dance instructor. I'd say all the evidence is in. Assimilate much?"

"How can you jump to so many conclusions? You haven't even met the guy yet."

"You never gave me that opportunity, did you? You know, I always thought your hard edge was an act, but it turns out you really are a—"

"Whoa. Don't say anything that I might have to slug you for later. All this over a wedding that you couldn't possibly want to go to anyway? After this is all over, we'll get the gang together, and I'll make it up to you. I promise."

After a long pause, Bass finally answered. "Only if you can fit us into your schedule."

Melody hung up the phone feeling like the biggest heel in the world. Bass had every right to be angry with her. She'd never blown him off like that before.

Mel physically readjusted her head, trying to jar it back into working order. After her relatives had really turned up the heat on the wedding-date interrogation last night, how could she have forgotten about Bass? Sure, most of their plans had been tongue in cheek, but she'd never given him reason not to make the obvious assumption that he was still invited.

She'd been so focused on Will lately, there had been little room in her mind for anything else. In fact, there was only one thing that had kept her from spending last night at Will's apartment. Stephanie had insisted upon sending a limo to pick her up, and Mel wasn't ready to reveal any part of her relationship until her family met Will at the reception.

Up until now, she'd continued her strategy of misdirection and deception to throw them off Will's trail. Her family could now only be disappointed when they saw how normal Will turned out to be. They would never believe a nice guy like that could see something in her.

Melody stepped into the shower, realizing how much she agreed with that sentiment. Ever since Will had confessed his love for her, she'd been asking herself just what someone like him saw in her. And more importantly, she didn't want him to change his mind.

Wanting to prove to him that she could fit into his world, she'd done just that. They'd worked out at his gym together, they dined at four-star restaurants, they'd even spent a day at the spa. And, although she was pretending to do all those things grudgingly, she'd never had more fun doing anything with anyone.

The truth was, she knew she loved Will, but she wasn't brave in the way he was. She couldn't bring herself to say it. If she put herself out there like that, he'd have all the ammunition he'd need to break her heart. As long as he thought she could take him or leave him, he might stay interested.

God forbid she actually start to count on him being there for her. One day, he might not be.

As she dried herself off, Melody studied her face in the mirror. She barely recognized herself anymore. It had been weeks since she'd lined her eyes with dark liner, and her most recent attire had been soft and feminine, instead of dark and grungy. She'd let Will pick out a few things for her, only because she loved the look he got in his eyes when he saw her in them.

Assimilate much? Bass's words screamed in her head.

She lifted her chin defiantly as she felt some familiar doubts creeping up on her. It felt good to be loved. And Melody refused to be ashamed of that.

* * *

Finally, they were standing outside the ceremony room of the Plaza Hotel, and it was just seconds before Melody had to walk down the aisle. She had been a rock. The most perfect handmaiden anyone could ask for. Fetching this and carrying that for Stephanie all day, trying to ebb the flow of her sister's nervous tears.

The wedding coordinator gave Melody her cue. She squeezed her sister's hand and whispered good luck as she left Stephanie alone to make her way down the aisle.

She had grudgingly participated in all the wedding activities up to this moment. She'd tried on three different iterations of Keenan's creations, until they'd settled upon these simple red silk sheaths that clung to each maid's slender form. She'd attended party after party where she'd endured questions about the suitability of her date.

Now as she marched down the aisle to a string quartet playing "Fleur de Lis," her eyes strayed to the left and found Will. He winked at her with pride.

She'd even paid half a month's rent to stay in this hotel which she thought was old and way overdone. But now, as she took her place at the altar, and watched the audience rise for her sister's entrance, it all clicked.

She got it—the reason people shelled out so much money and created this big spectacle. Tears welled in her eyes as she watched Keenan take Stephanie's hand and kiss it gently.

Love. It was nothing short of a miracle. People made as much fanfare as possible in telling the world they'd found true love, because it was just *that* big a deal. The enormity of it all washed over her. In a world full of misguided crazies, how was it possible for two people to fall in love...*with each other*...at the same time? Suddenly it seemed like an overwhelmingly impossible task.

Melody stole a glance at Will. He claimed to love her. But how did two people know it was going to last forever?

What made people brave enough to stand before God and all and declare such a thing? Melody admired Keenan and Stephanie, because she didn't know how she could ever be that certain.

Will had had many reservations about attending Stephanie's wedding with Melody, but now that he was there, he was actually having a good time. He'd gotten a big kick out of seeing her walk down the aisle in that tight-fitting red dress. He'd been informed that the bridesmaids, except for Melody and her youngest sister, were models, but none of the professionals had anything over Melody's natural beauty.

The only thing missing was Melody's hair swinging around her waist. The hairstylist had pulled it tightly back from her face into a shiny updo. Nothing like the sexy curly mass it was when she'd done it herself—it looked like it had been shellacked into place, impenetrable to the forces of nature.

This evening had proved to be a source of new insight into Melody. She'd said she came from wealth, but Will hadn't realized to what extent until he attended the wedding. The entire venue dripped opulence, the likes of which he'd never seen.

New York's elite in politics and fashion surrounded him. In fact, the business contacts he'd garnered at the cocktail party alone could catapult his career to the next level.

With a gut punch of clarity, he realized that Melody had been born into the life he'd spent years trying to achieve. He couldn't fathom turning his back on all of this.

In fact, he could see himself becoming a part of it. He'd already made a good impression on Melody's parents. They'd seemed a bit stunned when he'd first arrived at the table and introduced himself as Melody's date. But Beverly Rush quickly recovered her composure and turned on the charm.

Despite their obvious differences, Will was startled by all the similarities he noticed between Melody and her mother. Beverly was the source of Melody's elegant beauty, from her delicate bone structure to her catlike dark eyes. The women also shared an air of strength and single-mindedness. Beverly controlled all the conversations around her and deftly steered things to her liking. Will noticed so much of Melody in Beverly that he couldn't help liking the older woman, despite knowing Melody would view that sentiment as disloyal.

But it was Nathaniel Rush, Melody's father, that he'd bonded with most. They'd immediately become locked into a spirited debate over the current state of the stock market.

"Nathan, I do this for a living. Trust me on

this one," Will said in the face of the older man's stubbornness.

"Son, I've won and lost more money in the stock market than you'll ever handle in your lifetime. My experience tells me—"

"Experience is what's going to get you into trouble. Listen…" Will trailed off when he saw Nathan's gaze rise above his head.

He turned to find Melody gaping at the two of them in horror. "Wow, here I thought I'd made the safe choice for a date, and I find you arguing with my father. I thought you'd at least make it to the entrée before that happened."

Will rose to kiss Melody on the cheek. "You look gorgeous," he whispered in her ear as he pulled her chair out for her.

Beverly Rush positively beamed. "What a gentleman. There's nothing like a man with old-fashioned manners."

"Don't worry, sweetheart," her father said. "We weren't arguing. Just having a little difference of opinion. When your boy gets to be my age he'll realize—"

"Father, that's enough. I promised Will he wasn't going to have to talk business tonight. If you want to hear Will's opinions on the stock market, call him at the office and pay his fee."

Will felt his cheeks warm, not wanting Melody's family to think he'd stoop to soliciting their business, but before he could protest, Nathan stretched his hand toward him.

"Give me your card, kid. I'm willing to put my money where my mouth is."

As Will handed Nathan his card, he squeezed Melody's hand under the table. He couldn't wait to have her all to himself later that night.

Melody smiled back, and Will, momentarily forgetting his surroundings, started to lean in to kiss her.

"It looks like things are getting serious between you two," Beverly interrupted. "How long have you been dating? Melody has been very sparse with the details."

Will leaned back in his chair feeling like a deer in the headlights, and he could see Melody was about to open her mouth with a smart remark.

"Leave her alone, Mother." Melody's younger sister Vicky had arrived at the table with her young date in tow. He was tall and lanky, looking awkward in his ill-fitting suit. "You promised not to embarrass us in front of our dates."

Beverly looked aghast. "I wouldn't dream of it. I'm just trying to get better acquainted with William."

"Uh, it's just Will," he corrected. "My father used to say, with our income, we could only afford the first four letters."

Will felt his face heat for the second time that evening. He couldn't believe he'd volunteered that information—especially in this setting. He'd always been very careful with the details of his childhood. Particularly when in the company of those from wealthier backgrounds. But, after watching the tension mount between Melody and her mother, he realized how lucky he'd been as a child.

What his parents hadn't had to offer in luxuries, they'd more than made up for in unconditional love.

Beverly turned to Melody. "Well, at least tell me how the two of you met, dear."

Melody was spared having to answer her mother as the bandleader announced that the bride and groom would be dancing their first dance as man and wife. The room lights dimmed and the audience watched as Stephanie and Keenan glided around the floor. Immediately afterward, the bridal party joined them, and Will got the opportunity to appreciate his hard work first-hand.

Melody looked beautiful, and he was so proud when she resisted the urge to take over the lead when the best man faltered. The flurry of activity continued with the father-daughter dance until the floor was finally opened up to everyone.

That's when Will decided to take matters into his own hands. It was time to show Melody's family just how hard she'd been working over the last few weeks.

The fifteen-piece string orchestra began playing Frank Sinatra's "The Best Is Yet to Come," and he swept Melody into a jaunty fox-trot.

After their third spin, Melody whispered in his ear, "I don't think we're supposed to be upstaging the bride and groom."

"Nonsense, your family paid for those lessons, didn't they? We have to show them that they got their money's worth."

Melody just laughed and let him twirl her around the floor. They danced three more songs before the break for dinner.

As soon as they stepped off the dance floor,

several guests crowded around them to find out where she'd learned to dance so beautifully.

Will stepped back to enjoy Melody taking center stage. Finally, clearly embarrassed, she said, "Really, it's impossible not to dance well when your partner—"

"Has such natural grace," Will cut in. "Melody is so light on her feet, it's like dancing with a feather."

When the onlookers dissipated, Melody gave him a puzzled look. "You didn't want them to know you're my dance teacher?"

"Why spoil the illusion?" he answered, escorting her back to their table.

Melody was amazed that she was actually enjoying herself at Stephanie's wedding. She wasn't sure what she'd been expecting, but it had had something to do with a feeling of obligation rather than genuine fun.

It was as though she was living a dream, and in this ethereal world her mother was going easy on her, she was a fantastic dancer and she was loved by a successful businessman. Who would have thought any of those things were possible in her life, even for just one night?

And Will couldn't have been a more perfect date. He'd clung to her side all evening, making sure she wasn't thirsty or tired and gallantly helped her sidestep awkward conversation.

As the evening wore on, the guests began to thin and Melody found herself standing next to her sister.

"I think your dream wedding is officially a success," she said to Stephanie.

"And it wouldn't have turned out so well without you. I know it wasn't fun for you, but your full participation meant so much to me."

"Aww, it…it wasn't so bad."

"But you have to tell me, who is that gorgeous man you brought as your date?" She paused as her eyes went wide. "You didn't hire him, did you?"

From anyone else that would have been offensive, but from Stephanie it was merely comical. "Get serious. Believe me, if I'd gone to the trouble of such an expense, I wouldn't have hired Mr. Perfect over there. I'd come through with a showstopper like a fire-eater or the lead singer of Bad Religion."

"Of course, what was I thinking—that you'd actually do something to impress me? Must be all the champagne going to my head."

The sisters looked at each other and burst into laughter. "Okay, so where'd you meet him?"

Melody chewed her lip. "I don't want to tell you."

"Why not?" Stephanie gave her a wicked grin. "Was it somewhere nasty, like one of those S and M clubs?"

"Eew! What has gotten into you?"

"Come on, you'd better tell me. You know I'll imagine something much worse."

"He's my dance instructor from Moonlight Dance Studio."

Stephanie's jaw dropped. "You're kidding. You convinced him to come here and dance with you?"

Melody paused to give Stephanie an incredulous look. "No. We've been dating ever since the course ended. He's my *real* date."

Mel had known it would be a surprise to everyone for her to be seen with a clean-cut Wall Street man, but she found herself a little hurt at just how hard it was for everyone to believe.

"Wow, did I hook you up or what, girl! He's so hot."

"Yeah, he's okay. Just don't tell Mother. If she finds out that she's even indirectly responsible for my happiness…well, it would just ruin it."

"Okay, but be nice to him. He's the kind we all are looking for. Does he have a brother?"

Mel lightly punched her sister's arm. "You just got married, dummy."

"Ow, I didn't mean for me."

Just in time, Keenan walked up, ending their conversation. Melody took the opportunity to slip away to the ladies' room.

There was a line at least twenty women deep in the bathroom just outside the ballroom, so Melody traveled to a less crowded restroom on the next floor. As soon as she pushed open the door, her Aunt Thea's voice carried to her ears from one of the stalls.

"Now that was a sight I thought I'd never see—Melody Rush in a dress."

Melody stood there, unable to resist the urge to roll her eyes. It was just like her aunt to be caught talking about someone. What a shock that she was her present target.

"Well, I buy her dresses all the time. She just refuses to wear them."

Melody blanched at the sound of her mother's voice.

"I've been telling you all along, Beverly, that black fingernail polish mess is just a phase. I just knew as soon as that child found herself a good *Black* man she'd settle down. And just look at her with that big old handsome date of hers. Now you mark my words, this time next year we'll be doing all this for her."

Melody's ears started ringing as she took in her aunt's words. She braced herself for her mother's response.

"Well, it is quite a relief to finally see her with a man of our status. Clearly he's been a good influence on her."

Embarrassment and anger rushed up her neck like lava in a volcano. If she didn't get out of there she'd blow. And while she was sorely tempted to tell them how she felt, Melody ducked out of the bathroom before she could overhear anything more.

Chapter 11

"Melody, calm down, sweetheart. Better yet, let me help you," Will said, patting the space beside him on the king-sized bed in their hotel room.

He made an enticing picture, wearing nothing but dark boxer briefs, resting on a pile of fluffy white pillows with one arm behind his head.

But Melody continued to ignore him as she paced back and forth in front of the bed. "I don't know why I'm so surprised. Even though Mother complains about Aunt Thea being one of our 'ghetto' relatives, she can't wait to call her up when there's family gossip."

"It was a beautiful wedding, Melody. Everything turned out perfectly for your sister. That was your job. Don't spoil that by dwelling on a snide remark from your aunt."

"It wasn't just my aunt. My mother didn't exactly come to my rescue. It was the same with everyone. I knew they'd be a bit surprised, but why were they so damned…relieved? You know, 'I always knew you'd pull yourself together eventually.'"

Will burst out laughing, causing Melody to pause long enough to shoot him a withering look.

"I'm sorry for laughing, but if you could just see yourself right now. The reason you've always been comfortable being different is because you never cared what people think. Why should you start now? Especially since the reactions you've received have been of approval, not rejection."

"You're missing the point. Approval or rejection, that's not why I'm upset. Yesterday I was feckless and flighty because I like to wear black, listen to punk music and dated white boys with spiked hair. Today I'm stable and mature because my hair's in a bun and I'm dating a Black stockbroker."

Will shrugged. "And tomorrow you'll be feckless *and* mature because you'll be listening to punk music and dating a Black stockbroker. Who cares? Those are just stereotypes."

Melody nodded. "The thing I hate most about stereotypes is that people want to look at my skin or my clothes and say, 'I know you.' These people are supposed to be my family. They should know it goes deeper than that. I like that people have to work to get to know the real me. They have to earn it."

Will leaned forward, reaching for her. "Well, I'm not afraid of a little work. I'm ready to get to know you even better, and it starts with you getting out of those clothes."

"I'll be right back," Melody said, disappearing into the bathroom.

Once in there, she didn't hasten to get undressed. Instead she sat on the toilet seat to think. All night Bass's words had been playing in her head. Like a prophecy foretold, every time she was doted on by friends or relatives for how she looked, or danced or dated, she realized how far from herself she'd gotten.

Of course Will didn't think it was a big deal. Did he even know the undiluted Melody? He'd had her at a disadvantage from day one. He'd met her out of her element and off her guard. Somehow he'd snuck under the radar without ever facing the land mines and barbed wire of her defenses.

In fact, he'd never even seen her apartment. How could he claim to love her when he'd only seen a dim shadow of her true self? He'd yet to meet her friends or participate in any of her normal activities.

Melody stared at the bathroom door. She couldn't help wondering just how long this love would last if Will had to step out of the comfort of his own world.

Will started loosening his tie as he trudged out of the elevator Friday evening. He unlocked his apartment door, feeling so tired he could barely think straight. He really missed finding Melody on the other side of that door when he came home. Ever since the wedding she'd been opting to sleep in her own bed.

She'd wanted him to come over to her place, but that was just impossible during the week. She was all the way over on the Lower East Side, and he had to be at work by eight o'clock every morning. In fact, he was spending more hours at the office than ever before.

He'd had to call in a substitute for his ballroom dance class for that week, and now he was seriously considering quitting the side job altogether. Since meeting Melody, his career had really begun to take off. He'd run into Rob Geddes in the elevator at work last week, and for the first time, the corporate bigwig knew his name. The man indicated that he'd been following Will's progress, and if he kept up the good work, Rob had hinted that Will might be invited to join him for golf in the near future.

Things were really beginning to fall into place for him. He knew he was being watched at the firm, and the time was ripe to make some big moves. Will had spent Monday morning calling all the contacts he'd made at the wedding, and he'd locked down three solid commitments. The biggest of which was Melody's father. No pressure there; if he messed up that investment he could ruin his career *and* his love life.

But Will was up for the challenge. This is what he'd been grooming himself for all his life. Who knew a tattooed goth girl would be the lucky charm he needed to launch his career to the next level?

Thinking of Melody brought a smile to his face. Even though he was dead tired, he wanted to see her. He'd toyed with the idea of asking her to move in, but he didn't want to spook her. She seemed to shy away from commitment.

When he'd told her he loved her, he hadn't expected an answer in return. He hadn't been expecting a rush of tears either. That outburst of emotion told him everything he needed to know. She loved him back. Melody just didn't know how to handle affection.

She was so used to criticism and prejudice that unconditional love and acceptance startled her. He knew it would only be a matter of time before she became comfortable enough to express her feelings for him.

Feeling a wave of tenderness wash over him, Will picked up the phone. "Melody?" he said when she answered. "I really want to see you. How soon can you get here?"

"Why don't you come over here? I'm meeting some friends at the Black House later."

Will closed his eyes because he didn't have the strength to keep them open. "What the hell is the Black House?"

"It's a club. We're not heading over there until

ten. That gives you plenty of time to get down here."

Will could just imagine what type of club it was, and the idea of all that throbbing music when he was this tired made his head want to explode. "It's been a tough week. I was kind of hoping we could get some Thai food and sack out in front of the television."

"We always do that. Why don't you try something new for a change?"

"Sweetheart, I'm all for trying new things. I just can't today. I've been on the phone all afternoon trying to—"

"Yeah, sitting on the phone sounds really tiring. It's fine. You expect me to take the subway all the way up there every night, but when I ask you to come to me, you're too tired."

"Melody, look, it's not personal. It's just been a really hard—"

"I know, I work, too. Whatever. I have plans tonight, so I guess I'll see you when I see you."

Will stood staring at the receiver as the dial tone hummed. He had no idea how that conversation had deteriorated so quickly.

Shaking his head, he flopped down on his bed and fell asleep without even taking off his clothes.

* * *

Melody stared at the phone she'd just slammed down, feeling her body vibrate with fury. Hands on her hips, she simply stood staring at the phone and shaking her head.

Had she for one moment really expected him to come out with her and her friends? Of course not. What had she been thinking?

Their relationship only worked when she came to him—when she dressed the way he liked and participated in the activities he'd planned. Once. One time, she'd asked him to do something *she* wanted to do and he'd immediately rejected her.

"I knew it," she shouted at the phone. "I always knew you didn't really have an interest in me. Most people *want* to meet your friends. That is, if they're truly interested in you as a person."

Melody spun around on her heel and stalked away from the phone, trying to rein in her emotions. The clock on her cable box showed that she had four hours before her friends showed up.

But she had the urge to do something with the frantic energy bounding around inside her, something drastic that would fly in the face of Will's complacency with their relationship.

He'd never had to deal with her on a genuine

level because she'd held that side of herself back from him. That had been her own fault. Now she had to give him a giant dose of Melody Rush, full-strength.

At a quarter past ten her doorbell rang, and Mel was nearly finished getting ready. Pulling a fresh black T-shirt over her head, she jogged to the door.

Bass, Tha and Roland stood in the hallway. "Wow, a new look, huh? It's about time." Bass strolled past her into the loft.

Tha followed. "Sweetie, you should have told me you were coloring your hair. You could have done mine. I've been thinking about making the tips red."

"Black, platinum then red. That would be killer," Mel said, closing the door behind them.

"Why not, you already look like Cruella DeVil," Roland said.

"That's why you should totally do it," Melody answered. "Come over tomorrow and I'll help you. I still have plenty of red dye left."

Melody had fleetingly considered dying all of her hair crimson, but who was she kidding? She was way too vain about her hair to risk looking like an idiot. Instead she'd opted for a bold red streak in the front.

That alone had been a substantial effort. First, she'd had to bleach the strip of hair she wanted to color. Mel had almost stopped there, but it was too late to turn back and she wasn't prepared to walk around looking as if she was prematurely gray.

Finally after three washings and a laborious drying process, she was done. She hadn't had the time or patience for the flat iron, so right now her hair radiated from her head in big full waves.

With her black baby-T, she'd paired some red shorts and tights with black-and-white horizontal stripes.

Bass looked around the room. "Where's your man? I thought we were finally meeting him tonight."

"He bailed on me." Try as she might, Melody couldn't keep the bitterness out of her voice.

"Ouch." Bass threw himself down on the couch and propped his feet on the trunk Mel used for a coffee table.

"He was tired. He's been working a lot of long hours at the office this week." Mel couldn't help wincing. She sounded defensive even to her own ears.

"I'll try not to take it personally," Tha said, stalking to the kitchen. Her lightweight black coat dragged on the floor behind her.

"It's *not* personal. I'm sure he'd love to meet you guys. He just couldn't make it today."

Roland just shrugged, propping himself against the wall near the door. He was clearly ready to leave.

"Listen to yourself, Mel," Bass said. "I don't think I've ever heard you whine like this about some dude. Is he really worth all this trouble?"

Whining? Was she really whining? Melody felt her hackles rise. She snapped her fingers. "I have never whined about anyone ever. Don't get tart with me, Bass, just because I have a guy and you have no prospects on the horizon."

"That's actually not true. I'm pretty sure that model Lana had a thing for me. I was hoping to see her at the wedding but someone had to go and stand me up. You should definitely try to hook me up with her. You still owe me for that one."

Tha came back into the room drinking from a beer bottle. She leaned over the back of the couch. "That's right, Mel. You owe all of us the chance to watch Bass strike out with a model."

Melody rolled her eyes. "So that's why you

wanted to go to the wedding. Here I thought you were still carrying a torch for *me*."

Roland huffed from over by the door. "Can we get a move on please?"

They all gathered by the door and Bass leaned down to whisper in her ear. "When that stockbroker breaks your heart, you know I'm always here for you."

Melody sat at her drawing table, letting her pencil fly over her paper. Her publisher loved the new Ambassador story line, so she'd been spending a lot of time with Bass's face.

A week had passed since her confrontation with Will and Bass's disturbing pronouncement. At first she'd tried to reason that he was offering friendship in the face of a probable breakup, but reality had set in, and she knew that wasn't the case.

His gaze had been intense and even though he hadn't said anything more since, she knew he still had feelings for her. And, as awkward as that would be for their friendship, she found that knowledge completely comforting.

Since the wedding she'd spent so much time doubting herself. She was caught between two worlds, and she was torn between her family's expectations, Will's and her own. When it came to Bass, she knew where she stood. He accepted her. He understood her.

It had been two years since they'd dated, which hadn't been for very long. The truth was, she'd been a bit mean to him. She'd barked orders at him, and he'd run around doing her bidding.

Will never put up with her bad behavior. He viewed her mood swings as childish temper tantrums, and he never gave in to her angry manipulations.

In fact, that was why they hadn't seen each other in nearly two weeks. Whenever he'd called to get them together, she'd drawn a hard line in the sand. Every suggestion he made, she vetoed, replacing it with offers to come to her apartment or eat at restaurants in her neighborhood. Her rigid stance caused him to draw a hard, uncompromising line in return.

She was beginning to realize they didn't have as much in common as she'd originally thought. That had made her even more angry, and when they spoke on the phone, she showed him the full extent of her biting wit.

In her defense, she never set out to use her

anger as a weapon, it was an instinct that kicked in when she felt threatened. She had a tender heart that she would protect at any cost.

At least Bass understood that about her. That was why they'd been able to maintain their friendship. Now that they weren't dating, he didn't feel obligated to dote on her. And that was fine by her because, despite her bossy nature, she didn't like yes-men.

Suddenly the phone rang, interrupting her thoughts. "Hello?"

"Melody, it's Will."

"Yes, Will, I know your voice," she said coolly.

"Come on, let's stop this childish game playing. What we have is too special to throw away over a battle of wills. I'm ashamed of the way I've let my pride get between us lately. I'm willing to act like a grown-up. How about you?"

Melody mulled that over for a minute, the silence on the line stretching on.

"Oh, Melody, I know how much you love being angry, but let it go. Don't you want to have fun together again, like we used to?"

Her heart wasn't hard enough to withstand the rich timbre of Will's voice. The fact was he absolutely melted her with his words. Smooth to the core, he'd said all the right things, and she knew he meant them.

"Yes, I miss you."

"Yeah, now that's what I wanted to hear. I'm having Melody withdrawal with no kissing, no hugging, no loving."

"Okay, then come over here. I'll make it worth the trip."

Now the silence dragged out on his end. "I can't tonight. Before you get angry, let me say that I'm still at the office, and I'll probably be here a couple more hours." His voice became animated with excitement. "I think I'm on the verge of something big here. Geddes has really taken notice of the extra work I've been putting in and that golf invitation is inevitable."

"Good for you," Mel said flatly.

"The other reason I called is because there's a charity auction tomorrow to benefit one of Geddes's pet foundations. He invited me and a few other guys from the office to attend. I want you to come with me."

"Why? So I can sweet-talk the boss for you again?" She winced as soon as she'd said it. Clearly her mouth had a mind of its own.

"No, because I love you and I want you with me."

Melody felt terrible. She was behaving like a jerk and she was blowing what could have been the best thing that happened to her.

"Forget I said that. I'll be there." Melody suddenly wanted to be the bigger person.

Moving on impulse, she grabbed her purse and headed out of the door. Pride wasn't everything.

Chapter 12

It was ten-thirty when Will finally dragged himself in from the office that night. He'd been watching the work habits of the brokers who'd made big career moves at the firm, and it seemed they'd all done it by schmoozing the right company's heavy hitters, bringing in big clients and working long hours. He was trying to show them that he would do whatever it took.

But it was already getting a bit old. He hardly had time for himself anymore, and he knew his dedication to moving ahead was putting a strain on his relationship with Melody. She was feeling neglected. That had to be why she was suddenly challenging him at every turn.

He wanted to make it up to her, but he was so close to getting what he'd worked for all these years. If she could just hold on a littler longer—

"What the hell?"

Deep in thought, Will had made a beeline to the bedroom, loosening his clothes as he walked. He hadn't looked up until a movement on the bed caused him to nearly jump out of his skin.

Clutching his heaving chest he began backing toward the door as the figure reached out to turn on the nightstand lamp.

Will released a string of expletives for which his mother would have washed out his mouth.

"Will, Will, calm down, it's only me. It's Melody."

He was relieved to see Melody, but he'd been so startled, that his tired body was now too weak to do anything but sink to the floor. "Whew, well, thanks. Now I feel like a giant coward, freaking out over a woman in my bed."

She crossed the room to join him on the floor. "I'm sorry, I let myself in with the extra key you gave me. It was still light out when I came over, so I didn't turn on any lights. I must have fallen asleep until you came in. I stayed still because I was trying to surprise you. I didn't mean to give you a heart attack."

He reached out and brushed her cheek. "Now that I've recovered, I'm really glad you're here."

Will had been tired when he'd come home, but he had no memory of that now. He stood, reaching down to pick her up. There was one activity for which he always had energy on reserve.

It was late afternoon when Melody got home the next day. They'd spent the better half of the day lounging around in bed. She couldn't believe how tired Will had been. Normally, he hated to sleep in, but a herd of wild buffaloes couldn't have dragged him out of bed that day.

Not wanting to mess with the haunted kitchen, she'd run down to a nearby coffee shop for coffee and muffins while he'd slept. He'd been so groggy when he'd finally awakened, he hadn't even complained when she dropped crumbs in his bed.

Maybe she'd been unreasonable about his schedule lately. It was obvious that he was putting in long hours at the office because he was trying to move his career forward. Melody remembered what that was like. She'd taken any inking job for obscure comics she could get, just to get her name out there in the industry.

Dashing to the closet, Melody pulled out the dress Will had requested she wear. It was a slinky little number with spaghetti straps. The material faded from a smooth peach to a burnt umber at the asymmetrical hemline. The warm colors actually complemented the red streak in her hair nicely.

He hadn't commented on her hair color at all last night. But she figured that was because they'd been preoccupied with other things. Today, she spent a lot of time tucking the streaked hair back into a sleek ponytail so it was less emphasized. The evening was important to Will and she didn't want to let him down.

She was just strapping on a pair of low-heeled sandals when the phone rang. She was certain it would be Will checking up on her progress. He'd wanted them to take the same taxi over to the function, but she'd insisted on meeting him there to save time.

"I'm on my way out the door now," she said into the receiver in place of hello.

"Ooo-kay, I guess that means you don't want to see The Illness play tonight? I have an extra ticket," Bass said.

"Oh, Bass, I thought you were Will. I can't go out tonight. I have to attend some charity thing for his job."

"You two kissed and made up."

"Yeah."

"So he apologized for not investing himself in your lifestyle the way you did in his?"

"No…but he's been working so hard. He's been tired."

"I see, so he didn't apologize in so many words, but he's making more of an effort to accept the *real* you and not trying to dress you up as his perfect vision of a woman, right?"

Melody looked down at her clothes and her heartbeat sped up. "I know what you're trying to do, Bass, and it's not fair."

"What? What am I trying to do?"

"You're instigating. Sure, he asked me to wear a specific dress tonight, but that's because there are a lot of people he needs to impress at this function."

"And what? Your normal style isn't acceptable?"

"Stop it. That's coming from you, not Will."

"If Will truly accepts you, isn't it most important that you're there by his side to support him? Why does he get to pick out your clothes? Today it's a charity function, tomorrow a dinner party. It will always be something, and you'll have nothing to say because you let him get away with it."

Suddenly Melody felt very confused. She knew Bass was trying to manipulate her, but that didn't make his words any less true. When had she become the kind of woman who let a man dictate *anything* to her? Would Will really accept her as is, or did he need her to be the watered-down version of herself that she had become to make him like her?

After hanging up, Melody slipped off her dress and hung it back in the closet. Either Will accepted her one hundred percent, or not at all.

Will left the hotel ballroom for the fifth time, pausing to check his watch. Melody was late. He was just about to go back inside, when something caught his eye.

A dark figure was riding the escalator to the ballroom level. The first thing he saw was a pair of knee-high black boots with chunky heels. Will got a sinking feeling in the pit of his stomach as his gaze raced upward.

It was Melody. She was wearing a black corset with a gauzy layered black skirt that met her boots at the knee. Her lipstick was black. Her nails were black, and her hair fell in a long, straight cascade down her back with a shocking red streak in the front. Had that been there last night?

Will's body betrayed him, instantly becoming aroused. She looked pretty hot. But anger immediately tamped down that reaction.

The second her boots hit the carpet, Will was grabbing Melody's arm and leading her into a dark corner. "What the hell were you thinking?"

She looked him directly in the eyes. "I'm sorry I'm late. There was an accident on the road and the cab had to take an alternate route."

Will rolled his eyes in disgust. "That's not what I meant and you know it. Are you trying to embarrass me? What happened to the dress we decided you were going to wear?"

"You mean the dress *you* decided I was going to wear?"

"Whatever. Why aren't you wearing that dress?"

"That dress wasn't me. But this outfit is." She twirled around. "How do you like it?"

Will sucked in his breath. He almost never lost his temper. But she was toying with him. She was deliberately mocking him.

"This is a very swanky charity affair. You're not appropriately dressed."

"Wow," Melody said, looking down at her clothing. "I remembered you telling me once that you didn't care how I was dressed, you just wanted to see me. I guess that's not true anymore."

"Melody, at the time, you were meeting me at a bar. This is a private, invitation-only event that my boss invited me to. This isn't the time to take a stand in our relationship. This isn't the place to make some sort of…of crazy statement," he nearly shouted.

"Really? Because I've always believed that there's no time like the present. And you've just confirmed what I've been suspecting about you. You don't want to date Melody Rush. You want to date some weak-willed woman who you can dress up however you like and drag her around to all your charity events and fancy functions.

"All you care about is getting ahead in your

career. You never ask how *my* work is going. You've never seen the inside of my apartment or met even one of my friends. You're a selfish, self-centered jerk," she finished, poking him in the chest for emphasis.

Will stood frozen in place. His entire body throbbed with embarrassment and anger. He could feel the eyes of bystanders and all he could do was pray Robert Geddes wasn't among them.

"How dare you make such a big scene in public like this," Will gritted out through his teeth.

He saw Melody's eyes harden. "Well, you won't have to worry about me embarrassing you any further. We're done. You're not the man I thought you were, and I'm definitely not the woman you're trying to make me into."

She shouldered past him and headed back up the escalator. Will still couldn't move.

Melody sat at her art board sketching Will with fervor. It had been two weeks since their breakup and not a word had passed between them since that day in the hotel lobby.

At first she hadn't wanted to think about Will. She didn't let anyone say his name and she'd packed up all his pictures. But, now she'd found a new kind of therapy for a broken heart. She vilified him.

She'd discarded the superhero she'd been toying with to fight alongside Delilah. Now he would be a villain disguised as a superhero. She'd drawn Will's chin a little more chiseled than it really was, his teeth were a little bigger, whiter and straighter, and his eyes shone with the sparkle of diamonds.

He'd wear a sleek chrome-colored bodysuit, showing off his beautifully rippling muscles and his wide expansive chest. He was perfect. And his evil plan would be to rid the world of anyone who was different or unique by turning them into perfect clones of his design.

Melody indulged the wicked smile that curved her lips. She pushed down any guilty feelings that rose up when she thought about the millions of fans that would see this. Will would never know anyway. He'd never bothered to actually read one of her graphic novels.

The phone rang and Melody just stared at it. She really ought to invest in a few of the creature comforts that Will had introduced her to. Caller ID would come in handy right about now.

Every time the phone rang her heart leapt in her chest. For a split second, she'd wonder if it was Will. It was usually Bass, and she wasn't even that interested in talking to him anymore. He'd been giving her the hard sell ever since she broke up with Will, and the last thing she wanted was any sort of male companionship. She'd tried to explain that to him, but he thought persistence was a virtue.

Biting the bullet, Melody lifted the phone to her ear. "Hello?"

"Melody, dear, it's Mother."

"Yes, Mother, believe it or not, I recognize your voice. Despite the fact that you almost never call. Weren't any of the girls available for messenger duty?"

"Now, Melody, you know I really don't enjoy that biting wit of yours. I know it goes along with the culture of that whole gothic thing you were into, but it really is hurtful."

Out of courtesy, Melody simply rolled her eyes instead of scoffing aloud. "What can I do for you, Mother?"

"I wanted to invite you and William for dinner. Your father is very impressed with the way your young man has been handling his investments. It would be a nice opportunity for us all to get to know each other better."

"First of all, his name is Will. Just Will. He explained that to you at the wedding."

Beverly sighed. "I'm sorry, dear, but you can't expect me to remember everything."

"And second, we broke up."

There was silence on the other end of the line for a moment. "Did you hear me?"

"My goodness," Beverly said finally. "Well, you really shouldn't let someone like that get away, Melody. He was so good for you, and such a catch. Shouldn't you try to work things out with him? You can have quite the temper."

Melody's body turned to ice. She tried to swallow the lump rising in her throat. "That's really nice, Mother. You didn't ask me what happened, if perhaps he'd hurt *me* in some way. For all you know he cheated on me. Instead you automatically assume it's all my fault."

"Now, Melody, even if he did choose to keep company with another woman, you have to ask yourself if that's worth throwing away a good relationship."

Melody's jaw dropped as she resisted the urge simply to hang up the phone.

"Anybody else's mother would realize that maybe her daughter is in pain, and it might be a good idea *not* to pour salt on the wound. But, what was I thinking? My name isn't Stephanie or Vicky, so I'm not entitled to a little compassion, understanding or interest from my mother."

"You know that is simply not—"

"You've never accepted me for who I am. You've never even attempted to really know me. Instead, like some stranger on the street, you look at my outer appearance and you want to judge me. You don't care about what I'm like inside as long as I dress in your image and represent the Rush name."

Silence.

"Well, I think you've figured out by now that I'm never going to do that, so let's please just give up the charade. We don't have a relationship, and I'm tired of pretending. But cheer up, you still have two other perfect daughters. You don't really need *me,* do you?"

Silence.

Melody hung up the phone. And then she crumpled to the floor and sobbed. In that moment she'd had total clarity. Women were supposed to date in the image of their fathers, not their mothers, but she'd never been one for convention.

She let her heart pour out on the floor in the

form of her tears. She rarely cried, but now she released the emotions she'd kept jam-packed in her chest. The revelation she'd been fighting not to acknowledge washed over her.

Her mother didn't love her.

"Will, what are you doing here?" his brother asked when he opened the door.

"I could smell Frieda's hot wings all the way from the Upper East Side."

"Come on in. I thought you'd been making yourself scarce ever since you started dating Melody. When you gonna bring her around to meet us?"

Will threw himself down on the living room couch. "That's not gonna happen, bro. We broke up."

Tony released a soft expletive, drawing out the first syllable.

"There he is," Frieda said, coming out of the kitchen. "Hey, stranger," she said, leaning down to kiss him, still holding a pair of barbecue tongs covered in red sauce.

Tony turned to his wife. "You can set that extra chair at the table permanently," he said. "He just broke up with his girl."

She propped a hand on her hip. "Okay, now what did that hussy do?"

Will held up a hand to pause his sister-in-law's tirade. "I'm not sure exactly what happened, but I'm pretty sure she thinks it's my fault."

"Hold on, let me go turn off the oven."

Will looked around. "Where are the kids? Usually they would have come out of hiding by now."

"They're at summer camp."

Will's jaw dropped. "Are you serious? All three of them? How did you manage that?"

"It's actually pretty cool. I wish I could go. They're taught the inner workings of video games and how computer animation is done. Little Tony won a scholarship through his school, so they gave us a deal to send the other two."

"So you and Frieda have the place to yourselves for a while."

"Only for the rest of this week."

That's when Will noticed there were only two chairs at the table, and the unlit candles beside their good china.

He stood immediately, just as Frieda reentered the room. "I'm going to take off and let you guys relax."

"What are you talking about?" Tony asked, pushing him back down on the couch. "You didn't even tell us what happened."

"I can see the two of you were planning to make good use of your time without the boys. I don't want to interrupt."

Frieda waved him off. "Don't worry about that. You're here now. Talk to us."

Will stared at the carpet. "There's really not much to say. Ever since her sister's wedding, Melody had been more…edgy. She started picking fights about where we'd eat dinner and whose apartment we'd stay in. Things have been hectic at work, so I told her it's easier if we stay at my apartment. But she started refusing to come over, and she dyed this big red streak in her hair. Finally, she showed up at a work function looking like Morticia. She was trying to embarrass me. We had a very public argument about it, then she stormed out saying I should lose her number."

Frieda sat across from him twisting her rings. "So she changed after her sister's wedding? What was she like before that?"

"She was easygoing. She spent almost every night at my apartment. We went out to dinner all the time, went shopping and to the spa. She even helped me shmooze my boss at a cocktail party."

"So afterwards, she didn't want to stay at your apartment anymore?" Frieda asked.

"Right. She got bent out of shape because she said I didn't know what the inside of her apartment looked like. That I didn't know any of her friends."

Tony raised his brows. "Do you?"

"What?"

"Have you seen her apartment? Do you know her friends?" he pressed.

"I hadn't gotten a chance to do those things yet. I would have. I've just been really busy with work. Things are just starting to cook for me, if she'd just given me a little more time…"

Frieda stood. "I love you, Will, but I would have dumped your ass, too. You didn't even try getting to know that girl. You liked the relationship when it was convenient for you, but when she started demanding equal time, you bounced. I thought you knew better than that."

"Frieda, it's not as black and white as that."

Tony shrugged. "It sounds like it is to me. How much do you really know about how she lives her life when she's not with you?"

"I know a lot about her. I told you, she's a comic-book artist. She does *The Delilah Chronicles.*"

"Have you read any?"

Will felt his face heat as their words began to sink in. "No."

"So are you interested in working things out with Melody, or are you ready to move on?"

Will felt his anger resurface. "I'm really surprised you two are taking her side. She tried to embarrass me in front of my colleagues. Melody thinks our relationship is a game she has to win."

"We're on your side, brother, always," Tony said, squeezing his shoulder. "I just remember all the things you said you liked about her—she's sassy, strong-willed, not plastic like the other girls you've dated, not materialistic."

"Sounds like all the things you liked about her are the things you've been trying to change," Frieda added quietly.

"I'm not trying to change her." Will surged to his feet. "I'm going to leave you two in peace. Call ya later."

"Don't you at least want some wings to go—"

Will heard Frieda calling after him, but the door had already shut behind him.

Why didn't anybody see his point of view? His career was important to him. He couldn't let anything get in the way of that. Asking Melody to dress appropriately didn't mean he was—

As the elevator doors closed, Will sighed. Except for their last encounter, Melody had stopped wearing her funky collection of boots and those tiny tops that exposed the little tattoo in the small her back. She'd been wearing clothes he'd picked out for her and taming that gorgeous hair.

Ever since the wedding she'd been bursting to be herself again—and he'd refused to see it.

Will reversed the elevator and headed back up. "Do the boys have any of *The Delilah Chronicles* lying around?" he asked as soon as his brother opened the door.

Tony disappeared and returned with a big box filled to the brim with comic books. "I've been after the kids to get rid of these, but you're in luck, because they're still here. See what you can find in there."

Will dug through the box until he had a stack of twenty of Melody's books in his hand. "Thanks, you guys. I'm going to go and do my homework."

Chapter 13

Melody sat on the sofa with a pint of Ben & Jerry's Chunky Monkey, trying not to feel sorry for herself. She didn't even like ice cream. She rarely ate it. But this seemed to be one of those things girls did when they were depressed, and she was running out of options.

She was willing to do almost anything to fill up the giant void inside her. And the idea of packing it with ice cream actually amused her. Her very core would be sweet, but cold. The perfect way to attract men while protecting herself from their painful games.

The doorbell rang and Melody almost jumped out of her skin. It was nine o'clock on a Sunday morning. None of her friends would dream of being out and about this early. She wouldn't normally be awake herself, except for the fact that she'd slept so little the previous night.

She looked down at herself. She wore nothing but gym socks and a New York Giants football jersey. Reaching up she discovered her hair was a rat's nest.

Shrugging, she trudged to the door. She no longer cared to impress anyone. Looking through the peephole, Melody was surprised by the wave of disappointment that crashed over her as she realized it wasn't Will on the other side.

Unlocking the door, she pulled it open a crack and slogged back to her melting Chunky Monkey. Stephanie pushed into the room, and stood surveying it as though Mel were her daughter and she expected to find a man hiding in the closet.

"Why haven't you returned any of my phone calls?"

She shrugged. "Because I know why you're calling and I don't want to talk about it."

Stephanie surveyed her, hands on hips. "Maybe I wanted to show you my wedding pictures."

Mel looked up. "Okay, where are they?"

Stephanie crossed the room and made room for herself next to Melody on the sofa. "I didn't bring them."

Mel shrugged.

"Why on earth are you eating ice cream for breakfast? Do you know how bad that is for you?"

Melody shoved the pint into her sister's hands. "Fine, I'll go get a bottle of vodka instead."

Stephanie ignored her, clearly mesmerized by the ice cream. "I've never tried this flavor before."

"Go ahead and taste it. You're not modeling anymore. You're a housewife now, remember?"

Without hesitating, Stephanie dug out a big scoop and shoved it into her mouth. "Oh, my gahhh…" Her words dissolved into a series of moans that were only appropriate in the bedroom.

"Take it easy," Mel instructed, fearing her sister's eyes were going to roll back in her head.

Stephanie shoved ice cream into her mouth until the tub was empty. Then she stared into the container as though she'd lost her best friend.

"Great, you've eaten my only method of self-medicating. Now I'm going to have to go buy that black forest cake I saw in the deli window."

Stephanie snapped out of her daze, instantly remembering why she'd come. "Mel, you've got to call Mother. She's absolutely distraught over your last phone conversation with her."

"What a shame. I'm sure she'll get over it."

"Melody!"

"I'm serious. I'm tired of trying to please that woman. It's impossible. So I give up. Officially."

"That's not true, Mel. She loves you just as much as the rest of us. She's absolutely harassing Vicky and me to find out what's going on with you."

Melody shook her head. "No. No matter what I accomplish, no matter what goes right in my life, she only sees the negative. Now that I finally *could* use a little TLC, I can't deal with her heaping more crap on me. I need people in my life that already like me...for the way that I am, not for what I could become."

"Oh, Mel." Stephanie reached out and hugged her sister tightly. "You know that's how I feel about you, don't you?"

Melody nodded.

"Good, then start returning my phone calls. I'm

not Mother's spy. I'm here because I'm really worried about you." She gestured toward the empty ice cream carton. "So, is this about Mother or Will?"

"A little bit of both, I guess. No wonder they got along so well. They had the same method of trying to change me."

"Whoa," Stephanie said, staring at her sister as though seeing her for the first time. "I guess I was so caught up in the wedding that I didn't see it."

"What?"

"That you're in love with this guy."

Melody sat up straight. "What are you talking about?"

"Girl, you eat men for breakfast. They don't break your heart, you break theirs. But this guy really got to you. I've never seen you so much as flinch over anything a guy has said or done to you. But for this one, you'd try out an eating binge—also new."

Melody slumped. It was too much work to hide her feelings, and she no longer had the energy. Tears started trickling down her cheeks. "Will caught me off guard. I wasn't looking at him as a guy who wanted to date me, so I didn't have my defenses up. We had this really amazing attraction, and next thing I knew we were in a relationship. It just happened, and I didn't have time to shield my heart against him."

Stephanie squeezed her sister's shoulder.

"I thought he was different, and now I'm supremely disappointed. Mostly in myself for letting him in so easily."

Stephanie stroked Mel's hair. "It's okay. Believe it or not, this happens to the rest of us all the time. It's survivable, even though it feels like it's not."

Melody leaned into her sister, letting her cradle her. It felt good to finally let go and let someone else be in control.

Will wandered around the Penn Plaza Pavilion in awe. He'd never attended a comic-book convention before, but it was all he'd imagined and more. There were several fans dressed as their favorite comic or sci-fi characters, families, couples and individuals all milling about.

Will had spent the last week catching up on *The Delilah Chronicles*. He'd read the first one in an attempt to get into Melody's mind. He'd kept reading because he'd gotten hooked. He'd never anticipated that this form of fiction would appeal to him.

In his mind comic books were juvenile and one-dimensional, but he'd been so wrong. The stories were detailed and character-driven, and the addition of beautiful graphics made them more vivid and compelling.

After staying up late into the night plowing through comic books, he'd nearly missed an early-morning meeting at the office. Finally he'd hit a gap in the series and had found himself running around New York City to find the missing issues that he needed to complete it.

He'd tried to reach Melody for the last two days, but he'd received no answer. Finally he'd resorted to looking her up on Google and found her Web site. He'd had no idea she even had one.

That reality had washed over him like a tub of ice water. Melody knew everything about his job. She'd even met his boss and coworkers. He hadn't known anything about her passion. He hadn't known what a poignant gift for storytelling she had or what a truly brilliant artist she was.

Will had developed a new level of respect for Melody. From her Web site, he'd learned that she would be appearing at the New York Comic and Sci-Fi Expo this weekend.

He'd tucked the most recent issue of *The*

Delilah Chronicles under his arm and set out to find her. But that was proving to be more difficult than he'd expected. The expo was taking place in a gigantic room and there were tables upon tables of comic-book displays. He didn't know where to begin looking for the autographing sessions.

As the clock wound down, Will finally realized the signings were taking place on an entirely different floor. There were only fifteen minutes left in her scheduled appearance as he raced up the escalator.

Will found himself at the back of a very long line of fans, wondering if he'd be turned away before he got the chance to see Melody. It was strange now to be waiting in line to talk to a woman he'd been sleeping with every night only a month before.

He listened as her fans, mostly adolescent boys, chattered excitedly about meeting Melody in person. As he neared the front of the line he could hear what they said to her. And he saw an entirely different side of her. She looked the same, dressed in a black T-shirt, a denim miniskirt and her favorite army boots. Her hair was bound by cord into a long whip at the back of her head, with only the curling spiral of her sexy red streak flowing free.

But somehow, she appeared softer. She laughed with the fans, flirted harmlessly with the awestruck boys, posed for their pictures and generally accepted their worship with grace. And how they worshiped her, bringing her drawings they'd made in tribute and asking for her hand in marriage.

Will felt a ridiculous sense of pride as he saw how her fans treated her. She was amazing—he'd known that. But he hadn't known *how* amazing or how incredibly talented she was.

Finally, as the gangly young man in front of him stepped away, Melody looked up and saw him. For a split second, he thought he saw her eyes light up, then the light died.

"I didn't realize you were one of my fans," she said wryly.

"The biggest," he said softly. "Shame on me for not telling you sooner." He held out the comic book he'd brought over with him.

She studied the cover. "Did you actually read this?"

"Absolutely," he said proudly. "And all one hundred and twenty-seven issues that came before it."

She rolled her eyes as she signed the comic for him. "No, you didn't."

"Yes, I did. Test me."

She narrowed her eyes at him. "How did Delilah defeat the Wind Commander in issue forty-two?"

"That's an easy one, she trapped him in a subway tunnel."

"Okay, who did Delilah fight in issue ninety-nine, *The Enemy Within?*"

"She fought a clone of herself."

Melody rattled off a few more questions and Will wasn't stumped because he'd read all of her stories over the course of the last week.

"Okay, you win. I'm convinced." She tried to sound blasé, but Will could tell she was pleased. "So how did you know I was here?"

"I read about it on your Web site."

"You've been to my Web site?"

"Of course, I told you, I'm your biggest fan."

Their eyes locked for a few seconds, and Will felt like all was right with the world. All he had to do was ask her for another chance. She still loved him. He could feel it. And if he handled this situation just right, maybe she'd finally tell him.

"Are you ready to go, Mel?"

Will spun around and found himself facing a motley crew, led by a hulking man with red-streaked hair, wearing two layers of ripped T-shirts and skintight black jeans. Behind him was a thin preppy guy wearing makeup and a petite girl with half-black, half-platinum hair.

Melody stood. "Yeah, I'm all done here. Where do you guys want to eat?"

Will realized that Melody was about to walk away and that would be it. He couldn't let that happen.

He thrust his hand at the big guy closest to him. "Hi, I'm Will."

The guy just looked at his hand. "*The* Will?"

"Yeah, that would be me."

"I'm Bass," the guy said, finally shaking his hand.

"Oh yeah," Melody said, taking over the introductions. "This is Roland and his girlfriend Samantha."

"My friends call me Tha," she said, reaching out to shake his hand.

"Tha," Will tried the name. "I like that. It suits you. So where are you all headed?" Will asked, none too subtly.

"We're going to grab something to eat," Roland answered. "Do you want to come with us?"

"Yeah, I'm starving."

* * *

Melody sat at the fifties-style diner trying to take in a sight she'd thought she'd never see, Will Coleman sitting amongst her friends.

And to her surprise, they were actually getting along. She'd held her breath for a moment back at the convention center when Will had introduced himself to Bass. She'd had no idea what her friends' reaction would be to him.

But she'd worried for nothing. To her dismay, Will and Bass had instantly bonded. They were both from Brooklyn and enjoyed reminiscing about their favorite haunts.

And had Tha really blushed when Will said he liked her name? Since when had her friends become such pushovers? They were buying into Will's charm hook, line and sinker. Was she the only one who could see through the facade?

It certainly hadn't been her idea to invite him to tag along. So what that he'd read all of her work? It was just a cheap ploy to try and impress her. He'd play at being interested in her life for a minute then he'd be back to trying to change her.

She wasn't falling for it this time. And she really resented how her friends had changed sides so quickly. Didn't they realize she and Will had broken up?

"*Et tu,* Bass?" she said, shaking her head, realizing that, to her horror, Bass and Will were comparing notes.

"And she's such a control freak. Have you noticed that?" Bass asked.

"Have I noticed? Please, I bought a Tivo to catch all my football and basketball games. To this day, it's still recording *The Cartoon Network* almost exclusively because that's how Mel programmed it. When she stayed over, I wasn't even allowed to hold the remote control."

"Tell me about it," Bass said. "We once drove upstate to—"

"Okay, that is enough out of you two. You both were lucky I deigned to be seen in your company."

"You tell them, Mel." Tha sent a glare toward Roland. "Ungrateful bastards."

"What did I do? I'm just sitting here," Roland said.

Through the rest of the meal, Melody couldn't help feeling a little niggling of hope. It was like the first new growth of spring shooting through the hard-packed winter earth. And Melody took her giant combat boot and squashed it back into the ground.

She wasn't interested in getting her hopes up. That's why when Will offered to walk her home from the diner, she'd almost said no. But she agreed because she knew he was too much of a gentleman to let her go alone, and because it would be a good test of her resolve.

She'd let him in so easily. Free admission. The door was unlocked. No barbed wire or electrified fencing in his way. The entrance to her heart had been left unguarded. But it was guarded now, and she needed to be able to trust her own judgment again.

"So why did you show up at the convention center today?" she asked when they were finally alone.

"First of all, I needed to get issue one twenty-seven signed. I would have brought issues one through one twenty-six as well, but I thought that might have been overkill."

Melody stuffed her hands into the pockets of her denim skirt as she sped up to walk a bit ahead of him. "Is that the only reason?" She looked back over her shoulder so she could see his face when he responded.

"No. I started reading your comic books because I needed to feel close to you in some way. These last few weeks without you have hurt like hell."

Uh-oh. That little sprig of hope tried to poke through the dirt once more. But she couldn't start this cycle with another person. Was she really going to start things up with Will just to find herself years later still tying herself up in knots to win his approval?

She'd finally told her mother, enough was enough. She was free. She couldn't replace one pair of shackles for another. No matter how much a part of her might want to.

"So now you tell *me*," Will said. "Have you missed me at all?"

Melody swallowed. She waffled between the truth and a glib remark. She decided he deserved the truth, but she wasn't going to get all gushy about it. "Sure. We had a lot of fun together. I'd have to be made of stone not to miss that."

"Just fun?" He stopped her and pulled her to one side. "Am I crazy or did we actually have something? Something special?"

Mel sucked in her breath, pulling away to keep walking. "Whatever we had is over now."

"It doesn't have to be."

"It takes two people to have a relationship. And I'm out."

"Melody, I'm going about this all wrong. What I should be saying is that I get it. I know I didn't take the time to really immerse myself in your life. I always made you come to my apartment, my work functions, my favorite spots. And I'm sorry. Let me make it up to you. Let me really get to know the real you. I like your friends."

"That's nice, Will, but I'm out of the market for a boyfriend. I was never good at that whole thing anyway."

"Okay, then let me be your friend."

She snorted. "Yeah, right."

"I'm serious. Bass told me that the two of you used to date. So, why can't *we* be friends?"

They'd reached her apartment building now, and she had to give up the distraction of walking. "When did Bass tell you that?"

"When you were in the bathroom. So... friends?"

She hesitated. "It was different with Bass."

"Why?" he pressed.

Because I didn't love him.

"Because I knew Bass and I were going to be

running into each other. We hung out at the same places and were tight with the same people. It only made sense that we'd be friends. You and I are from different worlds. We could go our whole lives without seeing each other again."

"Okay. I understand." He turned and started walking away, throwing "Goodbye" over his shoulder.

"Goodbye," she said softly, startled by his quick departure. He'd given in so easily, she thought, as a coldness enveloped her.

Spring had slipped away, leaving her shrouded in permanent winter.

Chapter 14

Melody stared at her art board completely stumped. It had been a long time since a story line had eluded her. She was having one of those rare moments when she wished she were just the artist and someone else was responsible for the story.

But, she was in a unique position for a woman in the comic-book industry. She had complete control over her work, and with her deadline looming, she *had* to make something happen on the page. Hoping inspiration would come from thin air, she began to draw.

Her mind betrayed her as she attempted to show Delilah locked in a struggle with her new villain Platinum Man. The wrestling hold looked much more like an embrace.

Groaning in frustration, Melody was about to crumple up the sheet and start over, when the doorbell rang. Relieved to have an excuse to walk away for a while, Mel raced to the door. She flung it open, hoping Bass had dropped by to hang out.

She stopped dead in her tracks when she saw her mother standing in the opening. "What the—" Melody started and then she caught herself.

"May I come in?" her mother asked formally, looking very uncomfortable, clutching her purse with both hands as though she'd just waded through the jungle in her Ferragamo pumps.

"Actually, I'm working right now, Mother. Maybe if you'll just tell me what I can do for you…"

Taking a deep breath, Beverly Rush stalked past Melody into the apartment. "We need to talk. Our last phone conversation was very disturbing."

Melody shook her head, closing the door behind her. Of course the fact that she'd said that she was working didn't even faze her mother. The woman had never taken her work seriously.

Beverly perched on the edge of the sofa, still holding her purse with two hands, clearly uncomfortable.

Melody stood staring at her mother. She didn't want to sit down, too, because that might encourage her. She breathed in deeply, trying to brace herself. "What do you need to discuss?"

Beverly's face was tight, her lips pinched into a tense line. Mel had never seen her mother anything but confident. "I should think that would be obvious. You had a very unpleasant outburst the last time we spoke and you haven't returned any of my phone calls."

"Look, the last few weeks have been difficult for me, and I really don't need any grief from you on top of that."

Beverly shook her head, clearly confused. "I guess I'll just never understand why you won't even attempt to make an effort with me."

Melody stalked across the room. "*I* don't make an effort with *you?* Are you serious? You're over-critical and disapproving of my career, lifestyle and friends, and I'm the one who needs to make an effort?"

Her mother stared straight ahead, not meeting her gaze. "Yes, and quite frankly I don't know what else I can do about it. I invite you on outings that you turn your nose up at, you give away the clothes and gifts I buy for you. Yet I overheard you and Will discussing the spa and shopping at Neiman's. It's perfectly fine for you to do those things with him, but you won't consider them with me?"

Melody cocked her head. If she didn't know better she'd swear her mother was actually hurt. "Well, it should make you happy to know that I don't do those things with Will any longer, either. We broke up, remember? Besides, I never wanted to do any of those things with you because they were just your shallow attempts to make me over in your own image. If you can't accept and love me just the way that I am, then I give up. I'm done."

For the first time since her arrival, Beverly raised her gaze to Melody's. Were those unshed tears? The older woman blinked rapidly and they were gone. "If I didn't know better, I'd think you were trying to say that I don't love you."

A lump had formed in Melody's throat, surprising her with this sudden onslaught of emotion. She looked away, hearing her own voice quiver as she spoke. "Well, of course you love me…I'm your child. But, I know—I know that it's not to the same degree as you love Stephanie and Vicky."

"Good Lord!" Beverly dropped her purse, her entire body twisting to face Melody. "You really think that I love you less than Stephanie or Vicky? You think *that* little of me?"

Melody's head snapped up. Her mother was clearly angry.

"You don't have to defend yourself, Mother. Despite what myths society promotes, no parent is expected to love each child equally."

Beverly shot out of her seat so fast, Melody took a startled step back. "Melody! You're my firstborn. By far the brightest and most creative child I've raised, and you have the nerve to say that I don't love you as much? How dare you?"

Melody blinked, wide-eyed, as she stared at her mother in shock. She didn't move or even open her mouth.

"I know that we're not close," Beverly said more softly. "But you're strong and independent. You don't back down from anyone. I admire you so much. You're all the things I always wished I could be."

Mel's jaw literally hung open. "What?"

"I guess I never told you. If I had, maybe there wouldn't be this rift between us now." Beverly sat back down. "I do admire you. You don't play by anyone's rules and I've always wished I could be that brave."

Melody crawled on top of the trunk and sat on top of it with her knees pulled to her chest as her mother spoke.

"Growing up, we were the only African-American family in a white neighborhood. We were not wanted there and my parents made sure that we were shining examples in the community. We needed to prove that we belonged. That we were just as good as the rest.

"I had to dress properly, speak properly and act properly, because the moment I faltered I would disgrace my family. I always felt obligated to represent our race…to make up for every negative stereotype we bear. But, you—from the time you were a small child, you were headstrong. You were bubbling over with creativity. You couldn't paint without getting it from your head to your toes. I guess I was jealous even then. I had never been allowed to get dirty.

"And I knew that you resented me. It's funny that you accused me of not accepting you for who you are, because I always felt you didn't accept me. Everything that I valued you mocked and ridiculed as lame or frivolous. I don't suppose I gave you a lot of positive reinforcement growing up. But, to be honest, I didn't think you needed it. At least not from me. It was clear my opinion didn't hold value for you."

Melody felt her entire body go cold, and her face tingled with embarrassment. It wasn't until that very second that she realized how hard she'd been on her mother. She was right. The very things that had hurt her so much over the years were the same things she'd been guilty of herself.

Overwhelmed with the shame of her revelation, Melody whispered, "I'm so sorry, Mother."

Her mother nodded stiffly. "I'm sorry, too."

After the silence began to drag out, Melody met her mother's eyes. "So what do we do now?"

"We don't give up. Maybe we can finally start to really get to know each other." Her mother reached a hand out toward her.

Melody took it and held it firmly. "I'd like that."

Melody was just returning from the bar at Alchemy when she had a hallucination. Stopping short, still holding a beer in each fist, she blinked, trying to readjust her eyes.

Was that Will sitting at the table with her friends? In her absence two more chairs had been pulled up to the table, and that was definitely Bass sitting in one of them.

After being jostled from behind by a fellow club goer, Melody realized that she needed to keep moving. Roland was working late that night so she and Tha had expected to be on their own. Bass had made it known he was boycotting the new band Alchemy was featuring because they had crossed over to mainstream pop stations.

"What are you doing here?" she said to both men, setting the beer bottles on the table.

"Well," Bass piped up, "I decided to give BFD another chance. I heard they're looking for a Web designer and I told the bartender to give them my card."

"Ah, look who suddenly put capitalism ahead of his personal values."

She turned her attention to the man she'd been avoiding. She hoped her face didn't look as flushed as it felt. She hated herself for mentally reviewing her appearance—camouflage pants with a faded black tank and yesterday's French braid…yuck.

"And you? I didn't realize Alchemy was your scene."

Will looked up, giving her a casual shrug. "Bass invited me."

For some reason, Melody felt an irrational spike of anger. "So you two are hanging out now?"

Bass just shrugged and Will nodded. "I recently realized that I don't have a lot of friends in the city outside of work. Bass and I are finding that we actually have a lot in common."

"Will helped me make my first investment. I was telling him that I thought Marvel stock would be going up because they're making three new movies this year. Turns out I was right, the stock has already gone up since I bought it."

Tha reached up and tugged sharply on Mel's braid. "Ouch."

"Sit down. You've been standing there so long I'm tempted to hang my coat on you."

Melody plunked herself into the nearest chair, between Tha and Will. Suddenly she felt like the outsider as the conversation continued without her. A few minutes later, as Tha and Bass debated about whether or not the lead singer of BFD used to be in a boy band, Will leaned over to talk to her.

"Why are you so quiet tonight?" he asked.

As soon as she felt his breath on her ear, her whole body went hot. He was dressed simply in dark jeans and a very tight black T-shirt. He'd always had that way of looking good without even trying. She swallowed hard, planning to deny everything and found the truth blurting from her lips instead. "How am I supposed to get over you, if you keep showing up?"

His smile was neither smug nor humble. No, it was tinged with knowing pain. "Getting over me was your idea. Have you changed your mind?"

Not trusting her words, Mel simply shook her head. She'd made such progress in the last few days—getting through a night's sleep without erotic dreams, and she no longer needed to self-medicate with sweets—she couldn't throw all that away.

"It's okay," he said softly. "I'll wait."

And strangely enough, those words freed her to enjoy the evening. They didn't have to pretend there weren't feelings left on both sides. They would simply put those aside and try to be friends.

They had a good time at the club, and when Will offered to split a cab with her on the way home, she agreed, even though she knew they lived on opposite sides of the city.

"I'm glad the two of you are sorting things out," Will said kindly, after she'd described her emotional confrontation with her mother earlier that day.

"Yeah, we'll see how it goes. Next week I'm going to let her take me to lunch at Tavern on the Green, and afterwards, she's going to let me give her a tour of all the funky art galleries in SoHo. I'm sure it will be weird at first, but we're both committed to getting to know each other."

Will replied by reaching out to squeeze her hand tightly for a moment. Melody's pulse leapt into high gear.

When the cab driver stopped at her building, she invited Will up to her loft, fully intending to sleep with him.

Why not, she asked herself as they rode the elevator. People in movies did it all the time. One more for the road, right? It would prove that they could detach from each other.

Melody wasn't fooling herself with her twisted logic, but now that she'd gotten the idea in her head, she was unwilling to let it go. It had been too long since she'd felt his arms around her, and after those many restless nights, she figured she deserved a little satisfaction.

"So this is your place... I love it," Will said, taking it all in—not hard to do since it was all one room save the bathroom and her bedroom. "It's very you."

Melody, who was singularly focused on how to broach the topic of sex, didn't think twice as Will walked over to her art board. "What's this? Is this me?" he asked, lifting the sketch she'd last worked on.

Heat raced up her neck, and she swore softly. "Not exactly," she said, darting over to the board and snatching the drawing from his hands. But it was already too late and there were other drawings on the board.

He picked up a sketch she'd done to introduce Platinum Man. "This is definitely me. Am I a superhero?" he asked, unable to conceal his goofy grin.

"More like a super villain," she said, chewing her lower lip.

"Then why do you have us making out?" He gestured to the drawing in her hands.

"That's not me, it's Delilah and they're not making out. They're wrestling."

Will's wolfish grin was all the answer she needed.

"Give me that." Mel snatched the drawing from his hands. "It's not really you, you know," she lied, weakly.

He grinned. "Whatever you say."

They stared at each other for several long moments and something began to crackle between them. There was no time like the present, Mel thought, ready to make her move.

She cocked her head toward her bedroom. "So, do you—"

He was already shaking his head before she could get the words out. "Just friends, remember?"

She sighed. "I know, but that doesn't mean—"

"Not until you're ready."

Melody felt frustration welling up inside her. "What are you talking about?"

"You have to figure it out for yourself."

"What?" she asked stubbornly.

He reached out and gently tapped two fingers over her heart. "That I belong here."

Melody just stood in place as Will walked to the door and let himself out.

Chapter 15

Will prowled around his apartment on Sunday afternoon, unable to find joy in any of his normal pursuits. He didn't feel like watching the Yankees on his big-screen TV; he had absolutely no desire to watch the *Project Runway* marathon in the penthouse lounge with the rich and date-deprived; and he couldn't go back to Brooklyn again and face the perpetual look of sympathy on his brother's face.

He thought about the irony of that for a minute. Tony lived paycheck to paycheck with a wife and three kids to support. They didn't buy anything they didn't need, but the house was always clean and the food was always fresh and home-cooked. And they were happy.

Tony had always been happy because, in his own words, he didn't wish for anything more than he needed. But Will knew it was more than that. Tony had never taken any of the good fortune that came to him for granted.

Will, on the other hand, had always wanted more. More money, more respect, more status. He felt his face heat at the realization. How had he become so focused on the material? His parents hadn't raised them that way. His father had been a postal worker and his mother a cashier. They'd never had a lot of luxuries but the house had been clean, the food fresh and home-cooked and they had been happy.

And even though his parents were now retired in a lovely house he'd bought them in Florida, no longer needing to work their fingers to the bone, Will had been afraid. Afraid of living his life paycheck to paycheck and never having more than *just* what he needed.

Will felt shame wash over him. He'd never taken the time to really appreciate just what it meant to have all that you needed. In truth, he'd had more. His family was close. He spoke to his parents no less than once a week, he spoke to his brother nearly every other day, and they got together as a family either in New York or in Florida for every major holiday.

Watching Melody struggle to connect with her mother had finally helped him realize that growing up surrounded by material things didn't create a family. It didn't create love.

He'd spent so much time pushing to get more money, more respect, more status that he'd never stopped to notice he'd had those things for some time. Here he was surrounded by all that he'd ever wanted…and it felt so terribly empty.

He wanted to go to Melody right now, but he knew she wasn't ready yet. It had been clear that she'd wanted to make love last night, but afterward she would have had regrets. He wanted forever, not just one last hurrah.

In all the time Will had been living in the city, he hadn't met more genuine people than Melody and her friends. In his brief encounters with them, he'd enjoyed their biting wit and their passionate intellectual conversation.

Even though he was out to convince Melody

that he fitted into her life, the truth of that fact had never been so clear in his mind. Now Will just had to wait for Melody to catch up.

After Will rejected her invitation for a one-night stand, Mel spent a long restless night plagued with frustration and confusion.

She woke up bitter with no one around to take it out on. Finally, she called Bass for some answers.

"Ooh, what's wrong with you?" he asked, picking up on her tone immediately.

"How come you and my ex are suddenly best buddies?" she demanded.

"He came to me for help. I'm a good Samaritan, you know that."

"What are you talking about? You're supposed to be loyal only to me."

"Exactly." After a pause, Bass continued. "He seems like a good guy. Perfect for you, actually. I really admire how he doesn't take any of your sh—"

"Bass! I can't believe you'd sell me out like that."

"I'm not saying you have to spend the rest of your life with the guy, but he's serious about you.

Your problem is that you give up too easily. The minute someone disappoints you, you reject them before they can reject you. Will seems like he's in it for the long haul. He deserves a second chance. I think you should give it to him."

Melody didn't know how to respond. "Traitor," she said finally, before ending the call.

After her talk with Bass, Mel braced herself to see Will again. And sure enough, everywhere they normally hung out, Will was there. Her plan had been to ignore him, but that was nearly impossible. Melody kept waiting for the farce to grow old, but her friends seemed to genuinely like Will, treating him as if he'd been a part of the gang for years.

And, even though she knew she could be leading herself down the path toward destruction, Melody couldn't deny that she truly enjoyed Will's company—his witty jokes, his thoughtful manner and, of course, that hot body of his.

To his credit, he didn't paint his fingernails black or dress in costume to impress them. He showed up as himself, in his casual clothes, with his natural air of grace and masculinity, and that was all he needed to fit in.

The more Will fitted himself into her life, the

more Mel realized that she missed some of the things they used to do together. As much as she loved those greasy fries at their favorite diner, she found herself craving the lobster bisque from the five-star restaurant across from Will's apartment building.

She wanted to be honest with Will about her feelings, but she was afraid to take that chance. How could she be sure they wouldn't slip back into their old patterns, when the novelty of her lifestyle wore off for him?

Will had known that he was wearing Melody down, but nothing gave him more hope than her invitation to a luncheon where she was being honored. They'd spent a lot of time together over the last several weeks, but never alone and never at her request.

He felt incredibly honored to sit at the table with her entire family as the Association of Women in Publishing gave Melody a plaque to acknowledge her success in the comic-book industry.

Afterward, she had spent the rest of the day with him in Manhattan, walking the streets like tourists. He hadn't wanted their time together to end, so he offered to take her to dinner anywhere she wanted. She'd surprised him by choosing Beaux Rivage Supper Club in his neighborhood. She'd even worn his favorite dress to the luncheon—a slinky peach number that showed off her legs with its angular hemline.

Now as he drove her to his favorite ice cream shop in Brooklyn for dessert, he hoped she was ready to admit they were meant for each other. He couldn't take another day without holding, kissing and touching her.

"You've given me high expectations for this ice cream. Let's hope this place lives up to them," Melody said as Will held the door open for her.

"Trust me, you won't be disappointed."

Melody headed straight for the counter to peruse the flavors, but before Will could follow her, someone was calling his name.

He turned to see Frieda, Tony and the kids sitting at a table in the corner. Will froze, uncertain if running into his family was a good or a bad thing.

Melody appeared at his side. "Is that your brother?"

Accepting that fate had taken over, Will cupped her elbow and led her over to the table. "Melody,

I'd like you to meet my family. This is my brother Tony and his wife, Frieda. And these are my nephews—Anthony Junior, who is twelve, Reggie, who is ten, and this little man is Simon, who is seven."

Frieda leaped up to grab two more chairs from another table. "Melody, sit by me. I've been dying to meet the woman who gave this one a run for his money."

Will retrieved their ice cream orders and returned to the table, praying his family wouldn't put him on the spot. He didn't know where he stood with Melody yet and a little bit of pressure could break the fragile bond they'd been forming.

With that in mind, Will tried to direct the conversation. "Do you guys know that you're in the company of one of the nation's most notable women in publishing?" He went on to tell them about Melody's award, making her blush in the process.

"You're amazing," Frieda gushed. "I've seen the artwork in the comics the boys have had around the house. You're incredibly talented."

"I've read some of those comics," Tony added. "Your writing is just as good as the artwork. No wonder you're getting awards."

"All right, you two, stop it," Melody said, clearly embarrassed.

Anthony Junior looked at his brothers. "This is so cool, now we can tell our friends we know the creator of *The Delilah Chronicles*."

"Yeah," Reggie said, giving his older brother a high five.

"If you marry Uncle Will can we get free comics?" added the youngest.

"Simon!" Will held his breath, hoping Melody wasn't upset.

"I think we can work something out even without that condition," Melody said, laughing.

"That's enough. It's fine to congratulate Melody on her award, but you all know better than to beg for things." Tony admonished his kids, then turned to Will, rubbing his chin. "Wait a minute, I thought Hunting Hall Country Club was an hour away. How did you get back to the city in time for Melody's luncheon?"

Will blanched. "Uh no, you see, I, uh—"

But it was too late. Melody's head snapped up from her ice cream. "Country club? What are you talking about?"

"Uh, Tony—" Will tried to forestall him.

"Didn't Will tell you? He finally got invited to

that bigwig's golf game." Tony turned to Will, oblivious to his discomfort. "I thought your tee time was seven-thirty."

Melody blinked. "Today?"

"Yeah," Tony answered. "Don't keep us in suspense, man. How did it go?"

Will sighed. "I wouldn't have made it back in time."

All eyes were on him, especially Melody's. "You didn't go?" she asked in a whisper.

"I took a rain check. There will be other games."

After an uncomfortable silence, Frieda changed the topic, but Melody remained quiet, even as Will drove her home. He didn't know what she was thinking, but he took it as a good sign that she directed him into the parking garage instead of having him drop her off on the street.

As soon as they entered her apartment, Melody pressed her lips against his and began loosening his tie. Overcome with shock and joy, he surrendered to her ministrations for a moment, before grabbing her hands. "What are you doing?"

"I'm jumping you," she said, struggling out of his grasp and pushing his jacket off his shoulders.

He stepped back. "As much as it pleases me to hear this, I have to ask. Why?"

"Okay," she said, sighing, finally surrendering to his need to talk first. "All those times you told me that you loved me, I'm not sure I really believed you. But, now I know you must love me. Otherwise, why would you give up the one thing you've been working like a dog for these past months? Geddes finally invites you into his golf circle, and you decline so you can go to some dorky luncheon with me?"

Unable to help himself, Will wound his hand in her hair, letting the silky strands slide through his fingers. "I already told you, there will be other golf games. Geddes is known to golf at least once a week. How many times are you going to be honored by the AWP?"

Melody threw her arms around Will's neck and pressed her body against him. "I've been wanting to tell you that I love you—" her voice broke "—but I've been so scared."

Will let his hands glide up her sides. "I know you love me, baby. But it feels so good to finally hear you say it. I'm not going to let anything come between us again. Understand? No more running from our problems."

"You just try to get away, mister!" Melody pulled his earlobe between her teeth and nipped gently.

Will knew Melody was in a rush to unite their bodies, but he'd been waiting for this moment for so long, he wanted to savor it.

Guiding her into the bedroom, he pulled her into a close embrace, even as he peeled off their clothes. Once on the bed, he locked her in the frame of his arms and led her through their own private dance.

Her unrestrained murmurs of pleasure played like a string quartet in his ears, helping him choreograph their intimate tango. Slow, slow, quick-quick. Slow, slow, quick-quick.

When the music of their bodies reached a crescendo, Will let Melody take the lead, and he willingly followed her to their grand finale.

Epilogue

Melody's wedding day was all she had ever dreamed of and more. She and Will had planned it together down to the last detail, blending their tastes into the most creative event New York society had ever seen.

The ceremony had been held at a modest chapel in Brooklyn that Will's family had attended most of their lives. The wedding party was all dressed in black, each member wearing garments that best suited their bodies and personal style—a floor-length mermaid for

Stephanie, a sassy cocktail dress for Vicky and a black-on-black tuxedo for her man of honor, Bass.

They'd rented the Black House nightclub for the reception. Her favorite punk band Bad Religion had been procured to play the cocktail hour, and now a more traditional party band was announcing their first dance.

Will pulled her into a tight squeeze as they awaited their big entrance. "Are you ready?" he whispered in her ear.

She gave him a wicked grin. "You know me, I'm ready for anything."

"And now, for the first time as man and wife, I present to you Mr. Will Coleman and Mrs. Melody Rush Coleman."

Will escorted her onto the dance floor and they struck their starting pose. Melody had worked with her brother-in-law to design a traditional wedding gown with a Melody twist. Will swirled her around in a wide circle, then reached down to neatly tear away her hem, revealing a knee-length party dress.

Tossing the material aside, Will pulled her into frame and led her into their routine. Melody felt her emotions getting the best of her as she absorbed the moment. Cradled in Will's arms, she gazed lovingly into his warm brown eyes.

"Wait a minute," she whispered to him. "This isn't the song we've been rehearsing to. What is it?"

He smiled down at her. "It's a piece I had written for you. It's called 'Enchanting Melody,' because that's what you are."

As Will dropped Melody back into a steep dip, she could see all her friends and family surrounding them—her sisters, Bass and his date Lana, and her parents. As her mother beamed at her, Melody recalled her words following the ceremony. *This is the most wonderfully unique affair I've ever witnessed. I'm so proud of you.*

She cherished those words, just as she cherished this incredible day. Will brought Melody back up into his arms, and she pulled him into a loving kiss.

"I love you, Will. Thank you for being all that I wanted, and more importantly, what I really needed."

He smoothed her cheek with his hand. "And thank you for showing me that, every now and then, it's okay to trust love and let your partner lead."

* * * * *

*Turn the page for an exciting first look
at reader favorite Robyn Amos's
next Kimani Romance...*

LILAH'S LIST

Chapter 1

Multiple orgasms were among the many things she wasn't going to get to experience before turning thirty, Lilah Banks decided as she stared at her well-worn pink stationery. She hadn't seen her list since college graduation in 1999.

That day she'd crossed off *fall in love,* and neatly tucked the list inside her grandmother's antique jewelry box. The jewelry box had been packed up along with her other college memories, and had landed in the attic of the house she'd shared with her husband Chuck.

Until today, that box had remained sealed like Pandora's Box. When Lilah had opened it, all of her unfulfilled hopes and dreams had tumbled out with her American University sweatshirt and a ton of old photos.

Lilah had been a good girl and followed the rules. She'd married her college sweetheart, lost her virginity on her wedding night, and perfectly balanced her career in real estate with her duties as a domestic goddess. Yet here she was divorced after only six years of marriage.

She smoothed her hand over the list, studying the handwriting of a sixteen-year-old girl as it transformed into that of a young woman in her twenties.

At sixteen, she'd wanted to date Reggie Martin—never happened. At eighteen, rebelling against her goody-two-shoes image, she added *visit a nude beach* to the list—that did happen (spring break 1997). At twenty, the awakening of her social consciousness, she'd wanted to protest a worthy cause—but never did. And at twenty-one, the awakening of her sexual consciousness, came the thing about multiple orgasms.

Lilah shook her head. All the really *fun* things were still unchecked, and her thirtieth birthday was three weeks away.

"So much for that." She dropped the list to the floor and dug back into the box. She pulled out a framed photo of her kissing Chuck at the Kappa Alpha Psi fraternity cookout senior year.

Saving the frame, she tossed the photo into the waste basket at her right. Her world had been so different then.

At this point in her life, she'd expected to be preparing for motherhood instead of readjusting to single life. She should have been remodeling their fabulous three-story suburban home instead of unpacking her Georgetown condo after three months of living out of boxes.

The only part of her life that had stayed on track was her career. As a real estate agent she was at the top of her game, making more money than she knew how to spend. But, with her personal life so deep in the dump, it was hard to celebrate that success.

She plunged both hands into the box and pulled out the last picture frame. Lilah and her best friend Angie. They were lying on their dorm room floor, staring up into the camera she'd held above their heads. When the two of them were together, they were trouble. Their parent's had nicknamed them Lucy and Ethel because of their madcap adventures.

Angie was still Lilah's best friend, but they'd grown apart since college, and Lilah's marriage had had a lot to do with that.

After college Angie moved to New York to pursue her career as the next big name in fashion. Lilah had been certain she'd be spending a lot of time in the Big Apple visiting Angie, and had added a couple of New York-related items to her list. But, over the years, Chuck had always found reasons for Lilah not to make the trip.

Lilah bit back her rising anger over all the times she'd given in to Chuck's emotional manipulations. He'd been needy and insecure, and she'd been spineless and desperate to please. What a pair they'd made.

Her gaze dropped back to the two girls in the picture. Feeling a surge of wistfulness, Lilah grabbed her phone and began to dial. It was ten-thirty on a Saturday night, so the odds were strongly against her friend answering, but it had already been too long since they'd last spoken.

"Hello?"

"Angie, I'm so glad you're there."

"Lilah?" croaked a weaker version of Angie's vibrant timbre.

"Did I catch you at a bad time? You sound exhausted."

"It's never a bad time to talk to you, but I *was* running around the city all day looking for platinum buttons. Not gold. Not silver. Platinum—for some diva who doesn't let any lesser metals touch her skin."

While she was awaiting her big break, Angie was sewing costumes for an off-Broadway playhouse.

"Aw, honey, I'm sorry to hear you had such a rough day."

"Don't worry, as it turns out, Miss Thing doesn't know the difference between silver and platinum after all."

Lilah laughed. "You're so bad."

"That's why you love me."

"Anyway, I was finally unpacking the last of my boxes today, and you'll never believe what I found."

"Um, two million dollars' worth of gold bullion that you're looking to split with your best friend?"

"I found *The List*."

"The list? Oh, fifty things you wanted to do before thirty. Hey, your thirtieth birthday is next month. How far did you get?"

Lilah scanned the sheet, mentally crossing off a couple of things she'd accomplished in the last eight years. "I guess I'm almost halfway through it."

"November tenth is—" she paused for calculation "—twenty-one days away. Are you going to try to finish it off?"

Lilah huffed. "Some of these things aren't even possible anymore. Remember item number one—date Reggie Martin?"

Angie sighed. "Well, that one's not impossible. Just a bit of a challenge."

"Ha! Have you listened to your radio lately? Reggie Martin is even more unattainable now than when he was just your average high school stud."

Reggie Martin was the sole reason Lilah had made *The List* in the first place. Her father had been giving her some sort of pep talk about how anything was possible if she identified her goals and worked toward them. Sure, he'd been referring to things like college and career, but at the time, Lilah had been obsessed with Reggie Martin.

It had taken a great deal of self-restraint not to write *marry Reggie Martin* at the top of the list, but she'd decided to stay within the realm of possibility. He was the leanly muscled, baby-faced, track-running, future superstar that she'd tutored in math.

"I don't know," Angie argued. "I think we got you pretty close in high school. I had to bake Bobby Carnivelli cookies for two months so he'd let you take over as Reggie's math tutor. It's not my fault you were too shy to make the first move."

For her entire junior and senior years, she and Angie had devised one plot after another to get Reggie's attention, all of which stopped just short of her confessing her undying love. A girl had to have her pride.

"I'm old-fashioned. I prefer the gentleman to do the asking."

"Old-fashioned, my gluteus maximus. You were just a big fat chicken."

"Oh ho. Was I chicken in the sixth grade when I talked LaTonya Richards out of beating you up?"

"Well—"

"And what about the time I convinced a Maryland State Trooper not to give you another ticket? The ticket that would have ultimately caused you to lose your license. And—"

"I meant with boys, okay? You're a big fat chicken when it comes to boys."

"Fine. I'll concede on that point. Which brings us back to the issue at hand. Number one on my list, date Reggie Martin, has gone from unlikely to impossible. He's a superstar now."

Reggie had always been a singer. He had a lovely melodic voice. But no one could have predicted that he'd manage to parlay that into a career. Right now, his first single, "Love Triangle," was getting heavy rotation on all the air waves.

"He's not a superstar, yet—more like a rising star. It's not the same as trying to get a date with somebody like…Usher." Angie was eternally optimistic, which was one of the qualities Lilah missed most about her.

"Yeah, whatever, girl. Keep hitting that crack pipe."

"Okay, put number one aside for now. What else is left on your list?"

"Eat escargot, ride a mechanical bull, get a tattoo, crash a party—"

"Slow down there, girlfriend. Those are all things you can still do."

"Angie, I don't even *want* a tattoo."

"That point is moot. Listen…I have a plan—"

In the past, those four words between them would have given her a charge, but Lilah's mature, twenty-nine-year-old self had learned to avoid trouble at all costs. "No, *I* have a plan. How about we forget I ever mentioned the stupid list and talk about something else."

"Not a chance. Here's what I say. Come to New York a week before your birthday and we'll knock the list out."

"Remember number one—"

"I said I have a plan."

"You have a plan to get me a date with a hot new R & B singer?"

"No, I have a plan to get you a date with an old high school friend who happens to be a hot new R & B singer."

"Okay, let's hear it. This ought to be good."

"As I see it, we have two viable avenues by which to reach Reggie. One, I read that his older brother Tyler is his business manager, and he lives here in the city. We can try to contact him and enlist his help hooking up with Reggie."

Lilah remembered Reggie's older brother well. And she'd always been a tiny bit scared of him. If Reggie was sunshine, Tyler was a thunder cloud—a dark, brooding killjoy. During her tutoring sessions, Reggie had complained rather frequently about how hard his brother rode him. She'd always suspected Tyler was jealous of Reggie's talent and popularity.

"And the second avenue?"

"Well, you can't live in New York and work in the fashion industry without being hot-wired into the celebrity grapevine. With his brother managing his business affairs here in the city, odds are he either lives here or frequents the area. I know my contacts can dig up the dirt on his whereabouts. Then it's just a matter of matching the two of you up in time and space."

Sure, it sounded straightforward, even plausible, but Lilah knew from experience that their schemes never went according to plan. "Well, I have to hand it to you, Ang, that's not bad. You certainly haven't lost your touch."

"So we're on?"

"Not. A. Chance."

"What? Why not?"

"I have to work."

"I know for a fact you haven't taken any time off since the divorce. That was a year and a half ago. You must have vacation accrued up to your eyeballs."

"I just moved. There's still so much to be done around here."

"Nothing that can't wait."

"It's just not a good time…"

Angie was silent for a minute. "Wow, I guess your marriage really did crush all the life out of you. You've lost your sense of adventure."

Lilah gasped. That was a low blow. And it hit its mark. She'd been a good girl. She'd played by the rules. It hadn't made her happy.

She couldn't remember the last time she'd been utterly content. Her wedding day? College? She'd gotten so used to the status quo that she didn't even challenge herself anymore.

Her gaze fell back on the list. Maybe she needed to practice a random act of kindness. Maybe she did need to drink champagne straight from the bottle. She definitely needed to climb to the top of the Statue of Liberty and ice-skate in Rockefeller Center. She'd promised her best friend that they'd do those things together.

"Okay, I'm in."

Over the next week, Angie and Lilah talked nearly every day working out the arrangements for her visit. Lilah ended up taking off the entire two weeks before her birthday. After all, she was overdue for a vacation, and she'd need all the time she could get to work her way through the list. She'd booked a first-class flight—scratch that off the list—from DC to New York Friday morning.

Angie tapped into the grapevine and discovered that Reggie did, in fact, live in Manhattan. According to Reggie's bass player's wife's hairdresser, he was attending a private party in the Flatiron District Friday night.

"The party's at some trendy club called Duvet," Angie informed her the night before. "I Googled it and apparently they serve you food and cocktails on these enormous cushion-lined beds."

"Let's see—private party, Friday night, trendy club. Sounds like it'll be hard to get into. We could be waiting outside in the cold for hours— if they let us in at all."

"Oh, we'll get in. We have to."

"And why is that?"

"Because *crash a party* is on your list."

Chapter 2

Lilah's List, Blog Entry, October 27, 2007

I made out with a stranger last night. Yes, me, the girl who wears rubber gloves to carry trash cans to the curb, had my lips and tongue completely interlocked with a man I barely know. It's true, I've been in New York one day, and I've already succumbed to the debauchery. I wasn't fazed by the white-knuckle flight, the cab driver with a death wish or the cranky bouncer. But, put

me in a crowded room with a bed that sleeps
sixteen and a hot guy, and I completely lose
my cool. But, before you book me a ticket
on the next train to Skankytown, let me
explain.

When she'd boarded the plane for New York
that morning, Lilah had felt daring. Her blood
had pumped with excitement. Whether or not she
returned with a tattoo, a designer dress or a date
with a celebrity didn't matter. For two weeks she
was going to have fun, spend some much needed
time with her best friend and live on the edge.

She'd headed for her first-class window seat
only to find a gentlemen already occupying it.
Eventually, the stewardess was able to sort out the
mix-up, but that didn't keep Lilah from feeling
conspicuously like a fraud.

To make matters worse, the plane sat on the
tarmac for forty-five minutes while some unex-
plained mechanical trouble was investigated.
Thank goodness the flight was only an hour long,
because Lilah white-knuckled it the entire way.
So much for first class—it was lost in a blur of
fear and mimosas.

After struggling with her bags and arguing

with the taxi driver for trying to make a daring turn into oncoming traffic that had nearly killed them, Lilah finally arrived at the Casablanca Hotel. It was a self-proclaimed oasis in the heart of Times Square. She chose the place because *Casablanca* was one of her favorite movies. And watching it was one of the first things she was able to cross off The List.

She'd had romantic fantasies of sitting in front of the fireplace in Rick's Café and listening to "As Time Goes By" on her iPod. Unfortunately, she didn't even take the time to soak in the vibrantly-colored Moroccan decor. Instead, she flopped down on the king-size bed and slept like the dead all afternoon.

Lilah was just returning to a groggy consciousness when Angie began pounding on her door early that evening. "Take it easy," Lilah said, opening the door, heedless of her nap-mussed hair, wrinkled T-shirt and jeans.

Angie stood in the doorway, hand on hip, as she looked Lilah up and down. She clicked her tongue. "It's just as I suspected. So much to do and so little time."

Lilah blinked at her friend. "I love you, too."

Then she was swept off her feet as the taller

woman lifted her into a bear hug. "I'm so happy you're finally here. We're going to have so much fun."

Angie reached into the hallway for the suitcase she'd brought along, and bounded into the room, filling it with her energy. But, Lilah was feeling the opposite of energetic. Her days of staying up late and going out were long in her past. If the truth were told, she could get much more excited about room service and a movie rental than the agenda Angie was laying out for them.

"We have to get to Duvet early, otherwise we'll never get past the door. But don't worry, I have a foolproof plan to get us in."

"Great," Lilah said, falling back on the tousled bedsheets.

"Have you been sleeping all day?" It was an accusation.

"Yup," she answered without remorse. "I could barely sleep last night thinking about this trip. You know, the more I think about The List, the more impossible it seems."

Angie stopped rummaging through the closet to stare at her. "Since when do we let the impossible stand in our way? Two days before senior prom, when we were doomed to being each other's dates, it was your idea to storm the University of Maryland campus and ask every cute guy we saw to be our escorts. You had every girl at Richard Montgomery High School wondering how two nobodies scored dates with hot college boys."

"Yeah," Lilah said absently.

"You used to be fearless, remember? You could talk anyone into anything. What happened to you?"

When Lilah looked back on some of the stunts she and Angie had pulled in their youth, it blew her mind. She couldn't imagine approaching situations with the same reckless abandon she'd once had.

Lilah looked at Angie and shrugged. "What happened to me? I grew up."

After a few moments of awkward silence, Angie turned her attention back to Lilah's closet and began throwing her clothes around the room like a whirlwind.

"None of these clothes are acceptable for tonight's activities, and there's no time for shopping." Angie walked over to her suitcase and opened it up. "Fortunately for you, I came prepared. It's an original creation, and it will look stunning on you."

It was a burnt-orange, swirly-print cocktail dress with a complicated weaving of spaghetti straps across the back. It stopped just above Lilah's knees with a dainty flair. Lilah studied herself in the mirror. The dress was beautiful, if a bit bold for her taste.

"Good Lord, are those the only shoes you have?" Angie turned up her nose at Lilah's functional, decidedly non-designer black pumps.

"I'm afraid so, unless you think my pink Timberland's would work with this look."

"I guess the pumps are going to have to do. I don't know how you balance on those tiny pinpoints you call feet, anyway," she said with a comical glare that had the two of them bursting into giggles. Angie's feet were two sizes bigger than her own—and Angie all but hated her for it.

Lilah piled her light brown hair atop her head in one of those sloppy knots she'd seen in magazines. She was going for an air of elegant maturity. She silently prayed she didn't look the way she felt—like a little girl playing dress up.

Physically, Lilah hadn't changed much since high school. She still got carded on a regular basis. With her clear champagne complexion, no makeup and her honey-brown hair worn loose, she was a dead-ringer for sixteen.

It would be a few more years before Lilah felt being mistaken for someone younger could actually be flattering instead of mildly annoying. Her tiny, soft voice did nothing to help matters. That was why Lilah relied on makeup and a severe topknot to force clients to take her seriously. She also tried as hard as possible not to be bubbly.

Angie, on the other hand, epitomized bubbly. Add that to her two-toned Macy Gray fro and funky homemade clothes and people frequently underestimated her wickedly keen mind.

Angie in her typical statement-making fashion was wearing a skintight vinyl tube that passed for a dress. With this she wore black leggings and multicolored paint-splattered boots, under a long dark coat straight from *The Matrix*. With her orange curling Afro frosted at the tips, her hair radiated from her head like rays of sunshine.

"Okay, are you ready to hear my strategy?" Angie asked later, as they rode downtown in a taxi. The late-October night air had just enough bite for them to need overcoats, but it wasn't cold enough for gloves and scarves yet.

"I can't wait," Lilah answered, unenthusiastically. She wasn't looking forward to this adventure. In fact, considering the way her trip had begun, she was convinced this entire outing would be a disaster.

"Listen up, I have a three-tiered plan to get us past the doorman. Phase one, and the least likely to work, we flash our brilliant smiles and sweetly ask to be let in."

"If that's unlikely to work, Angie, why is it even part of the plan?"

"Because we're attractive women—we're armed with Mother Nature's tools. It never hurts to try them out."

Lilah rolled her eyes. "What's phase two?"

"We drop the high school connection."

"What?"

"We tell the bouncer we went to high school with Reggie Martin."

That gave Lilah a start. She hadn't seen Reggie since high school graduation. Would he even remember her?

She took a deep breath. Of course he would. She'd spent countless hours in his house for their tutoring sessions. He usually turned up an hour or so after she did, which gave her plenty of time to take in personal details and talk to his family about him.

And he'd been so nice to her. He always made sure she had a ride home with his brother whenever he couldn't take her himself. He would even confide in her about his family problems.

But what would she say to him after all these years? Suddenly the list sounded so juvenile. Hopefully he wouldn't laugh in her face.

"Please tell me phase three is a real winner. Otherwise, I suggest we turn this cab around and go have a nice dinner. I haven't eaten all day."

"Phase three is a sure thing."

"I'm listening."

"Filet mignon."

"You agree we should go for dinner?"

"No, that's the code word."

"What are you talking about?"

"Apparently, all bouncers know this code word. It means let us in immediately, we're very important people."

"And just where did you get this information?"

She pointed out the window. "Look, we're almost there."

"No changing the subject. Where did you hear this?"

Angie sighed. "The Internet."

Lilah's spine snapped straight. "Driver!"

Angie grabbed her arm and covered Lilah's mouth. "Shh. This is going to work. You'll see."

Lilah climbed out of the cab, her legs trembling ever so slightly. "This is going to be so humiliating."

Angie gripped her elbow and started marching her forward. "You know the drill. Say everything with confidence and authority, and you'll have those bouncers eating out of your hand."

They approached a tall, dark-skinned man with dreadlocks and a black leather trench coat. "Hi, we're here for the party," Angie said brightly.

The man frowned at her. "We don't open to the public until after midnight tonight. We have a private party going on," he answered with a thick Jamaican accent.

"That's right," Angie continued. "We're here for the party."

The man just shook his head.

"We're meeting our high school friend Reggie here. *Reggie Martin.*"

The man pointed over Angie's shoulder to the long line stretching down the block.

"What's that line for?"

"Dat's for everyone who wants to be let in after midnight."

"But, it's only eight-thirty."

His gaze remained cold.

"By the way," Angie said finally, "we're filet mignon."

The bouncer glared at her. "Really, 'cus you look more like chopped liver." He turned to Lilah. "And this one barely looks over eighteen. Don't try flashing dem fake IDs 'round here. I can spot 'em a mile away."

"Now wait a minute," Lilah said, finally finding her voice. "There's no need to be rude. I realize you probably hear a lot of creative stories from people trying to scam their way into the club. And I'm certain it's no fun to have people approach you like they own the world and expect to be treated like it. But you don't look like the kind of gentleman whose mother raised him to disrespect women."

Lilah resisted the urge to giggle at the look of wide-eyed chagrin on his face. "I...uh...I—"

"Please tell me you're not giving my friends a hard time," a deep masculine voice called out behind them.

Lilah froze in place. She knew that voice. It couldn't be—

She turned and found herself looking up into a pair of brown eyes. He towered over her at well over six feet and was dressed in a black winter coat over an impeccably tailored dark suit. His crisp white shirt was open at the collar.

All of Lilah's words stuck in her throat.

"Mr. Martin, my apologies," the bouncer said, opening the rope for them to pass through.

Chapter 3

As he guided the two women past the entryway, Tyler Martin was pleased to have done his good deed for the day.

He hated velvet ropes, bouncers, celebrity parties and all the air kisses and fake smiles that went along with them. Helping these girls get past that thick-necked jerk redeemed some of the self-respect he'd lost profiting from this life.

But, on second glance, Tyler realized that he recognized these women. He'd be hard-pressed to remember the name of the tall one with brightly-colored hair, but he'd know Lilah Banks anywhere.

It was hard to forget the shy sixteen-year-old who had sat at the kitchen table with him more times than he could count.

"I know you two, don't I?" He touched Lilah's arm. "You're Lilah Banks, right?"

Lilah started. "You know my name? You remember me?"

"Of course. You spent so much time at our house, our housekeeper thought you lived there."

Lilah laughed nervously and her friend stepped forward. "I'm Angie Snow, Lilah's best friend."

"Oh yes," Tyler said, shaking her hand. "I recognized your face."

He'd been two years ahead of the girls in school, so he was already in his first semester at the University of Maryland when Lilah started tutoring his brother.

His heart had gone out to her because it had been so obvious that she'd had a huge crush on Reggie. More often than not, she'd been stuck with *him* because his younger brother had his head in the clouds and rarely showed up for tutoring on time.

When Reggie *had* shown up, he wasted her

time bitching about how hard things were around the house. Hard? The kid had everything handed to him on a silver platter. It was Tyler who picked up the slack. Shopping for food, running errands and driving the tutor home while Reggie played video games in his bedroom.

But, if Reggie was self-centered, he had no one to blame but himself. Their mother was a doctor and their father a lawyer. So, although they always had every new gadget and video game, their parents were rarely home. Vivian Martin didn't like having strangers raise her kids, so when Tyler was old enough, Reggie became Tyler's responsibility.

Thank God he loved the kid. Which wasn't difficult since Reggie had a witty sense of humor and was genuinely fun to be around. He had an inherent charm that made it easy to forgive his mistakes. They were extremely close, which worked out well since their worlds were so tightly intertwined.

Reggie had a natural gift for music and Tyler had a natural gift for business. While Reggie wrote songs in the recording studio, it was Tyler's job to handle the business details, including making sure the accountant, publicist and the rest of the industry didn't take advantage of his baby brother.

Which brought him to his present situation. He normally avoided the limelight whenever possible, but he'd come to accept that in this business, important meetings often took place in the VIP lounge of some popular nightspot. He now represented several people in the entertainment industry, and tonight Reggie wanted him to meet a potential new client.

Now that he'd gotten them past the doorman, Tyler half expected the girls to float off. Instead, they huddled close, with no obvious agenda.

The room—lit with pink, green and orange neon lights showcasing wide decadent beds with drapes and pillows—was buzzing but not packed. He scanned the area for Reggie, but since he didn't see a crowd of fawning females, he knew Reggie wasn't in the room.

A DJ pumped mellow dance music through the speakers, loud enough to catch a rhythm but not so loud as to discourage conversation.

"Um, you're probably wondering why you found us trying to crash this party, huh?" Angie started.

"Since you mentioned it, yeah."

"Well, we're kind of on a mission. Tell him, Lilah."

Lilah blanched and gave her friend a stunned glare.

Tyler tried to break the ice. "Like a scavenger hunt?"

Lilah gulped. "Yeah, sort of. Um, when I was sixteen I kind of made this list. A list of things I wanted to do before I turned thirty."

Tyler nodded. He was thirty-two, which meant the big three-oh had to be just around the corner for Lilah.

"My birthday's in two weeks, and I thought it might be nice to finish off the list."

"And something on your list involves this club?" Tyler couldn't help noticing that Lilah seemed perfectly mortified. He wanted to ease her embarrassment, but he didn't know how. He didn't even know what she was trying not to say.

"A couple of things, actually." She pulled a PDA phone out of her purse and showed him the illuminated screen. "Crash a party and…uh, something else."

"What's the other thing?"

"It's actually pretty convenient that we ran into you because it involves your brother Reggie," Angie said, trying to help Lilah along.

"Ahh, I see…" He should have known.

If it were possible, Lilah seemed even more embarrassed. "Keep in mind, I started this list when I was sixteen." She scrolled her PDA screen and handed him the phone.

Item number one on her list was *Date Reggie Martin*. For some reason that Tyler couldn't define, his heart sank.

He'd known she'd had a crush on his brother back in the day. He'd even tried to get his brother to acknowledge Lilah's interest in him, but Reggie had insisted that Tyler was reading too much into the situation.

Lilah rushed to explain herself. "I know it sounds absurd. He probably has a girlfriend or fiancée or something. I just thought, maybe, as a favor to a high school friend, we could have drinks or something. That way I can cross this off my list with minimal intrusion in his life."

Tyler couldn't help himself. He threw his head back and laughed. When he saw the hurt expression on her face, he immediately brought himself under control. "I'm sorry. Yes, he's single. I'm sure I could arrange some sort of meeting that would qualify as a date."

Lilah was visibly relieved and Tyler felt his

stomach muscles clench as she asked, "Is he here tonight? We heard that he might be here."

"Yeah, he's supposed to meet me here. He's probably in the VIP area, wherever that might be. Hold on."

Tyler pulled out his cell phone and punched the speed dial number for his brother.

"Yo," Reggie answered with his standard greeting.

"Where are you? I'm at the club and I don't see you."

"I'm downstairs in the VIP room. Come down."

"Actually, I'm up here with a couple of women who would like to talk to you."

"Nice. Brother, you work fast. Are they hot?"

Tyler let his gaze slide over to the two women watching him expectantly. He turned his back, feeling heat creep up his neck. "Of course."

Angie, tall and willowy with her wild explosion of curls, was definitely beautiful, if you liked that funky art-student vibe. Lilah, on the other hand, was petite and curvy with luminous pale skin and honey-colored hair. She hadn't changed much since high school. In fact, if he hadn't known better, he would have sworn that she was *still* in high school.

The only really noticeable change were her eyes. They no longer held the open invitation he used to see there. Now, they were clearly marked "Do Not Disturb." She'd been burned by someone.

But, then again, who hadn't? It was only a matter of time for most people anyway.

"Do you want me to bring them down?"

"Nah, if they're the clingy type, once they're in, I'll never shake them off. I'll come up. Give me ten."

"Great. We'll get a table…er, bed and wait for you."

He clicked the phone shut and turned back to the girls. "He'll meet us up here in ten minutes. I'll see about finding us a spot to hang out."

Angie shook her shoulder so hard, Lilah thought her arm might fall off. "See, this worked out just like I said it would."

Lilah snorted. "Not even close to how you said it would. Besides, it hasn't 'worked out' just yet."

"Come on, what are the odds of Tyler Martin coming to our rescue of all people? For a split second, I actually thought it was Reggie coming up behind us."

"You're not the only one." Lilah decided that

it was her state of shock that accounted for her sudden loss of breath at the sight of Tyler.

Her memory of him hadn't done him justice. She'd gotten the basic stats right in her mind's eye—tall, dark-skinned, the same chestnut brown eyes that Reggie had. But, the real beauty lay in the details.

He was so much taller than she'd remembered. Sure, she was only five foot two, but Tyler seemed to loom in the night like a dark tower in a black overcoat. And his skin was dark, but it glowed like burnished wood—clear and smooth.

And those light brown eyes were not so much brooding as she'd remembered, but intense. He'd always looked at her as though he could see everything inside her. Like she was emotionally naked before him. It was one of the things that she'd always found so disturbing about him.

She'd never thought of Tyler as handsome—certainly not compared to Reggie. But her memory had gotten that one wrong, too. He was definitely handsome. Not in the smooth-faced, curly-lashed, flash-those-pearly-whites way that Reggie was good-looking.

Tyler had a face that was well put together. A strong jaw with just the hint of stubble, a nose that was pointed without being too sharp, deep-set eyes and thick lips and with hair rounded into a tight, businesslike fade.

Sexy. The word flashed in her brain and was gone, like a subliminal ad.

"We gotta get some drinks in you," Angie said, tugging her arm. "You're so nervous you're practically catatonic."

"I'd rather have some food. I'm starving."

"This place is also a restaurant. I'm sure we can get you something, eventually. The drinks are necessary now. We have to make sure you can actually speak when Reggie gets up here. You're so stiff, you could be made of cardboard."

"We can't leave. Tyler's coming back for us."

"Fine. You wait here. I'll hit the bar. You still like Appletinis, right?"

"Yeah, that's fine." Lilah's mind had already wandered off. In a matter of minutes, she was actually going to be talking to Reggie Martin.

She saw Tyler's tall dark form emerge from the crowd. He came to her side, taking her elbow in his hand. Leaning down to her ear, he whispered, "I'm going to take you to bed."

Chapter 4

Lilah felt Tyler's breath on her ear as he spoke, and his words registered with a jolt. *I'm going to take you to bed.*

She jerked back from him, off balance from the unexpected erotic thrill tingling the base of her spine.

Tyler reached out and steadied her with both hands, preventing her from reeling back into a passing waitress with a tray full of drinks.

"I'm so sorry," Tyler said, as she pulled herself together. "I should never have said that. I didn't mean to startle you. I was just trying to be clever. That was inappropriate."

"No, no. It was fine," she tried to reassure him, feeling foolish for getting so flustered. "I can take a joke."

"Why don't we go sit down?" He looked around. "Where's your friend?"

"Angie went to the bar. Will she be able to find us if we get in be—uh, sit down?"

"I'll make sure she does," he assured her.

He began steering her toward one of the large beds along the far left of the room. A waitress helped them settle in by tucking their shoes in a drawer below the bed and giving them each a pair of terrycloth slippers emblazoned with the word Duvet.

Just as Lilah was awkwardly climbing onto the mattress, Angie arrived with two green apple martinis. Tyler helped Angie juggle the drinks as she took off her boots and joined them on the bed. Lilah and Tyler had checked their coats, but Angie insisted that hers was an integral part of her ensemble.

Lilah quickly discovered that it was hard to recline comfortably and keep her dress from riding up. She finally arranged herself into a suitably modest position, wishing desperately that she'd worn pants.

"I'm not sure whose idea this was—" Angie started.

"I know. It's the worst," Lilah chimed in.

"—but I love it," Angie finished at the same time.

"You don't like it? I think it's great." Angie was propped against the row of cream satin pillows with her long legs stretched out in front of her. Her long jacket draped her legs.

Tyler looked right at home, too. He was stretched across the bottom of the mattress giving him plenty of room for his legs as he propped his head on his palm. He would also have a bird's eye view of Lilah's underwear if she forgot herself and moved her legs.

"What brings you ladies to New York?"

"I live here," Angie answered. "I design costumes for a playhouse in Greenwich Village, and Lilah's just visiting for the next two weeks. We've got to check off the rest of her list before November tenth."

Tyler nodded. "That's a pretty ambitious task. How many things have you gotten done since you got to New York?"

Lilah chewed her lip. "I flew in this morning,

first class. That was one. And we crashed this party. That was two."

"So what's this big soiree for anyway," Angie asked, sipping her martini, and then placing it back on the clear doughnut-shaped table for drinks in the center of the bed.

"It's a corporate launch party for a new men's cologne called Isosceles." He pointed toward the center of the room, and Lilah noticed for the first time that there were large pyramid displays of triangular cologne bottles.

"Since Reggie's single is called *Love Triangle,* his publicist thought this would be a good opportunity for some cross promotion."

Lilah's heart sped up. "Will Reggie be performing tonight?"

"No. He agreed to make an appearance and sign copies of his single. He convinced a few of his boys to tag along, so I don't think he's planning to hang out here long."

"Damn, sounds like there aren't going to be a lot of other big celebrities here then?" Angie asked.

"No, I've seen a few Broadway actors and radio personalities, but for the most part this crowd is media types and corporate investors. It's safe to say that Reggie is probably the most famous person here."

Lilah felt her stomach growl and took a sip of her drink because it was the only thing on the table. "Aren't they supposed to have food here? Do you think we could get a menu?"

"The waitress told me that the restaurant is closed. They have some cold hors d'oeuvres and sushi, but I think that's it."

Lilah wrinkled her nose. She wasn't in the mood for anything cold. She wanted hot food in healthy portions. Forcing herself to relax, she took another sip of her drink. Reggie would be coming around shortly. After she pleaded her case to him, she and Angie could leave and get a real dinner.

"Are they giving out free samples of that cologne?" Angie wondered aloud. "Those little bottles are cute. I think I'm going to go over there and try to snag one."

Angie bounced through the crowd, leaving Lilah and Tyler alone. Lilah tilted her glass and drained the last of her apple martini.

Her head started to swim as the drink finally began to work on her empty stomach. Great, the last thing she needed was to be plastered by the time Reggie showed up.

But, on the upside, she was suddenly feeling one hundred percent less anxious than she had been just five minutes earlier. She leveled her gaze at Tyler, who had directed his attention to the plasma screen in the center of the room.

"Do you ever get back to the DC area?" she asked.

He turned to face her. "Not often. Our parents still live there, but since Reggie and I both live here, they prefer to come up."

"I guess that makes sense." Lilah tucked her feet under her body and leaned forward, smoothing her dress across her knees. "How did you both end up here? Did Reggie come first and you followed him?"

"No, after I graduated from the University of Maryland, I came here to attend law school at Columbia. After trying his hand at a lot of day jobs, Reggie finally gave up and moved up here with me. Eventually, he made some connections in the music business and the rest is history.

"I guess you could say I've been his business manager all his life, but in the last couple of years, it started taking over. I finally decided to manage him full-time, and recently, I started taking on other clients."

"You both must be doing very well."

"What about you? You still live in DC?"

"Yeah, I just bought a condo in Georgetown."

"What do you do there?"

"I'm in the real estate business."

"That's great. How do you like it?"

"It's fine." Her answer came out like a half-hearted sigh.

Suddenly the fact that she was a very successful real estate agent didn't seem to count for much. Especially when she was surrounded by all these sparkling happy people.

Without thinking, Lilah reached for Angie's martini and gulped it down.

The fact remained that she was about to be thirty and her life was nowhere near where she'd expected it to be.

Time was bearing down on her like a freight train, and she was stalled on the tracks.

"Tyler?" The warm-colored lights straining through the canopy's filmy curtains and the effects of the Appletinis made her feel like she was in a cocoon. She felt secluded, despite the fact that there were clusters of people on the canopied beds all around them.

"Yes?"

"I'm going to be thirty in two weeks." Her voice shook with emotion.

He chuckled. "Okay, but you shouldn't worry about it. You don't look a day over eighteen."

She pursed her lips. "Why does everyone think it's a compliment to say that to me? I'm not a little girl. I'm a woman." Whew and she was *drunk!*

Lilah could hear herself and knew she sounded ridiculous, but she was powerless to stop.

"I can see that," he said huskily. "Trust me, no man in this room would mistake you for a child."

Lilah felt her face light up with embarrassment. His gaze had rested on the daring décolletage of her slinky dress. This conversation was definitely headed in the wrong direction.

And it wasn't just the conversation. *She* was headed in the wrong direction. Seeing Tyler reclining on the end of the bed, taking her in with his hooded gaze, sent a pulse straight through her.

In her inebriated state, she was quick to remember just how long it had been since she'd been in proximity of a good-looking man and a bed. She had a sudden wacky impulse to climb on top of him.

But two drinks hadn't made her bold enough to do that. Her survival instincts were still intact. "Do you think Reggie will notice?"

Tyler straightened into a sitting position. "Of course, in fact, let me find out what's keeping him." He took his cell phone out of his jacket. "I need to find a better signal. Be right back."

Lilah didn't watch him walk away. The room was spinning. She lay back against the pillows and closed her eyes.

Tyler swore under his breath. Contrary to what many outsiders believed, tonight was the first time in history that Tyler had been jealous of his brother.

As a general rule, he and Reggie weren't even attracted to the same type of women. It's not that Reggie was particular. He wasn't. He liked them all shapes and sizes. On more than one occasion, his younger brother had tried to offer Tyler his leftover groupies. Tyler always refused.

He had a more discriminating eye. Easy and available wouldn't do for him. They had to be sophisticated, ambitious and intelligent. But, he was a man. He liked them sexy with curves, too.

As a result of the brothers' differing needs, the two never fought over women—or anything else for that matter. Reggie wanted fame. Tyler just wanted success. Reggie wanted to make music. Tyler wanted to make money. They were like yin and yang. Perfect opposites, which made for a balanced relationship between them.

Until now.

For the first time, Tyler felt himself coveting something that wasn't meant for him. Lilah Banks had walked into his life and captured his attention entirely. For the first time that he could remember, he'd been about to indulge in a serious public display of affection. And from the look on Lilah's face, he was certain she was on the same page.

Only the Martin man that she wanted was his brother.

So be it, Tyler told himself. He wasn't hard up for dates. He'd been casually seeing a lady attorney for the past few weeks. The best thing for him now was to find his brother and leave the rest to Lilah.

He no longer wanted to be involved. Stepping

into the corridor leading to the bathrooms, Tyler speed-dialed his brother.

"Yo."

"Where are you? You said you'd be up in ten minutes. You know what? It doesn't matter. I'm just going to bring the girls down to you, okay?"

"Uh, actually, bruh, me and the boys are at the 40/40 Club. I was just about to call you. Why don't you grab the girls and meet up with us here?"

"Are you kidding me? You left without telling me? Why would you do that?" Tyler tensed. He was ready to launch into a lecture on wasting other people's time.

"The boys were getting bored. We had to roll out quick so we wouldn't get caught by the fans. I didn't have time to come upstairs. The manager let us out the back door."

"You could have called me. The only reason *I'm* here tonight is to meet your friend. What happened with *that?*"

"He's here. Don't trip. Just meet us."

"No, I'm done for tonight. Later." Tyler clicked the phone closed before his brother could respond. His anger would ebb quicker if he didn't have to hear Reggie's voice right now.

Great. Now he had to go back to the girls and tell them they'd crashed this place for nothing. Oh well. He'd done what he could. Now he just wanted to get home and take a shower. Preferably cold.

As Tyler crossed the room, he saw that Angie seemed to be on the receiving end of an intense sales pitch from one of the Isosceles promoters. Climbing the steps to their bed, he froze, taking in Lilah's prone form.

Sleeping Beauty.

Her face was burrowed into one of the satin pillows and her feet were curled beneath her. Hair slipped out of her updo to trickle down her neck. For a fleeting second, Tyler had the strong urge to curl up beside her and kiss her awake.

He shook it off. He wasn't Prince Charming in this fairy tale. That role was reserved for someone else.

Moving over to Lilah's side, Tyler gently lowered his weight onto the bed, careful not to startle her. He leaned over her, and softly prodded her shoulder. "Lilah. Wake up."

She murmured under her breath and rolled onto her back. Her eyes fluttered open and she gave him a sleepy smile.

"Lilah, I—"

She grabbed his lapel and jerked him downward. Tyler found himself sprawled across Lilah's body. Then she kissed him.

Wide-eyed, Tyler remained as still as stone as Lilah's lips explored his. Feeling his ardor resurface, he groaned in defeat, and took over the kiss.

He didn't believe in PDA, but no man in his right mind could resist this. She was soft and warm, and her lips had the faint tart taste of green apples.

His tongue surged into her mouth, and when he finally broke the kiss, she moaned in protest. "Reggie..."

Tyler's spine snapped straight and Lilah's eyes cleared. She was no longer lost in her sleepy alcohol-induced haze. Her eyes were filled with shock and confusion. She opened her mouth to speak...

Slipping his hand behind her neck, he kissed her with persuasive force. He felt Lilah's arms curl around him as she leaned into his embrace. Finally he pulled back to look into her eyes.

"My name is Tyler. And I don't want you to ever make that mistake again," he said, just before his lips found hers again….

* * * * *

Make sure not to miss the
entire publication of
LILAH'S LIST by Robyn Amos
available from Kimani Romance
January 2008

Every smart woman needs a plan!

DOWN AND OUT IN
FLAMINGO
Beach

National bestselling author
MARCIA KING-GAMBLE

Joya Hamilton-Abrahams's plan was simple: make a short visit to Flamingo Beach to give her ailing granny's failing quilt shop a makeover—then hightail it back to L.A. and civilization. Settling down in the small town was never on her agenda...but neither was falling for hunky construction worker Derek Morse.

Available the first week of May wherever books are sold.

KIMANI
ROMANCE™

www.kimanipress.com

KPMKG0160507

You can't hide from desire...

A GUILTY AFFAIR

National bestselling author

Maureen Smith

Journalist Riley Kane has long suspected that the death of
her fiancé—a San Antonio police officer—was not a simple
accident. So she reluctantly enlists the aid of his former
partner, Noah Roarke. But the sizzling desire surging
between Riley and Noah fills them each with incredible
longing...and unbelievable guilt.

Available the first week of May wherever books are sold.

KIMANI™
ROMANCE

www.kimanipress.com

KPMS0170507

Sinfully delicious and hard to resist...

Can't Stop LOVING *You*

Favorite author

LISA HARRISON JACKSON

Kaycee Jordan's new neighbor, pro athlete turned café owner Kendrick Thompson, was as irresistible as the mouthwatering desserts she created. When he agreed to help build her bakery business, days of work gave way to nights of luscious pleasure...until their relationship caused a rift between their families.

Available the first week of May wherever books are sold.

KIMANI™
ROMANCE

"The prolific Griffin's latest story pulls at the emotional strings..."
—*Romantic Times BOOKreviews* on
Where There's Smoke

BETTYE GRIFFIN

LOVE
for All Seasons

Alicia Timberlake was the woman of Jack Devlin's
dreams, but Alicia had always kept people at a distance,
unwilling to let anyone close. Still, Jack isn't about to give
up without a fight. But when a family tragedy reveals a secret
that makes Alicia question everything she's ever known,
she's suddenly determined to reassess her life and learn,
finally, how to open herself to love.

Available the first week of May
wherever books are sold.

ARABESQUE®

www.kimanipress.com

KPBG0100507

A soul-stirring, compelling
journey of self-discovery…

journey
into My Brother's Soul

Maria D. Dowd

Bestselling author of
Journey to Empowerment

A memorable collection of essays, prose and poetry,
reflecting the varied experiences that men of color face
throughout life. Touching on every facet of living—love,
marriage, fatherhood, family—these candid personal
contributions explore the essence of what it means to
be a man today.

**"*Journey to Empowerment* will lead you on a
healing journey and will lead to a great love of self,
and a deeper understanding of the many roles we
all must play in life."—*Rawsistaz Reviewers***

Coming the first week of May
wherever books are sold.

tangled
ROOTS

A Kendra Clayton Novel

ANGELA HENRY

Nothing's going right these days for part-time
English teacher and reluctant sleuth Kendra Clayton.
Now her favorite student is the number one suspect in a local
murder. When he begs Kendra for help, she's soon on the road
to trouble again—trying to find the real killer, stepping into
danger...and getting tangled in the deadly roots of desire.

"This debut mystery features an exciting new
African-American heroine.... Highly recommended."
—*Library Journal* on *The Company You Keep*

*Available the first week of May
wherever books are sold.*

KIMANI PRESS™

www.kimanipress.com   KPAH0680507

Celebrating life every step of the way.

YOU ONLY GET *Better*

New York Times bestselling author

CONNIE BRISCOE

and

Essence bestselling authors

LOLITA FILES
ANITA BUNKLEY

Three fortysomething women discover that life, men and
everything else get better with age in this entertaining
three-in-one anthology from three award-winning authors!

Available the first week of March wherever books are sold.

KIMANI PRESS™
www.kimanipress.com   KPYOGB0590307